## A Bloodthirsty Temptress

In spite of the light pressure she'd used while she was holding her weapon to Longarm's bare skin, the tip of the blade carried a small drop of blood with it when she brought it up. Belthane glanced at the shimmering red drop, then returning her gaze to Longarm and keeping their eyes locked, she lifted the knife to her mouth. Her tongue darted out and licked away the blood, then she pursed her full red lips into a budded smile.

Longarm had seen evil in human eyes before, but that which was carried by Belthane's glance was more sinister than any he'd yet encountered.

—◆— TABOR EVANS —◆—

# LONGARM

## AND THE QUIET GUNS

JOVE BOOKS, NEW YORK

LONGARM AND THE QUIET GUNS

A Jove Book/published by arrangement with
the author

PRINTING HISTORY
Jove edition/June 1988

ISBN: 0-515-09585-0

Jove books are published by The Berkley Publishing Group
200 Madison Avenue, New York, New York 10016.
The name "JOVE" and the "J" logo
are trademarks belonging to Jove Publications, Inc.

PRINTED IN THE UNITED STATES OF AMERICA

10  9  8  7  6  5  4  3  2  1

# Chapter 1

"How much farther you figure we'll have to go, Relimee?" Longarm asked. He peered ahead into the gathering twilight, trying to see through the tangled scrub and having little success. The high-growing leafy brush and the darkness created barriers far too dense even for his keen eyes to pierce.

"Not very far," the young woman riding beside him answered. "I don't really get lost in this underbrush, but it all looks so much alike at night that I can't say within a mile or two exactly how far we've come."

"It sure ain't been easy riding," Longarm commented. "And the nags are getting tired again. Suppose we pull up and give 'em a few minutes' rest."

"We might as well," Relimee agreed. "We won't be able to see the shack where Brennan and his partners are meeting until we break out of this thicket, so a few minutes won't matter too much."

"I reckon," Longarm told her as they reined in. "It might even be a help to us if we lagged a little bit. We're making as much noise as a Fourth of July band concert on the town square. If Brennan or any of the others are on the way there, chances are they'll be keeping their ears cocked. They couldn't keep from hearing us."

"But don't forget that they'd be making as much noise as we are. Even if they hear us, it's likely they'd think we're a deer or a strayed steer going down to the water to drink."

"Oh, even if I didn't say anything about it, I already

figured on that, just like I reckon you did when you led us into this miserable brush patch."

As he talked, Longarm had been sliding a long thin cigar from his vest pocket. He brought out a match and scraped his iron-hard thumbnail across its head, then shielded the tiny flame with cupped palms while he puffed the cigar to life. When the cheroot's tip was glowing red, he held the cigar between his thumb and forefinger and cupped his hand around the glowing tip to keep it from flashing a signal through the fast-gathering darkness to anyone who might be within eyesight.

While he was lighting up, Relimee had been looking around, trying to find a familiar landmark, but in the twilight dimness one patch of undergrowth looked like every other patch.

"I still don't think anybody could hear us without us hearing them," she observed. "At least that's what our old men say when they talk about hunting or about the days back in the East, when our people were still fighters."

"Not till we'd get out of the brush," Longarm observed. "And chances are all of them fellows have already gotten to that cabin you've been telling me about. You sure about how much farther we've got to go?"

"Reasonably sure." Relimee nodded. "Something like another quarter of a mile ought to see us out of this scrub growth and close enough to the sand spit where the rivers join."

"Maybe Billy Vail was right about not sending me on this job," Longarm said before he clamped his strong yellow teeth down on his cigar and nudged his horse ahead with the toe of his boot. "Somebody from the west Arkansas district that knows the territory might've been better. I feel pretty much at home most places in the Indian Nation, but this just ain't one of 'em."

Longarm had made much the same observation to Billy Vail when the chief marshal had called him into his private office almost two weeks ago.

"You'd better put two extra shirts into your saddle-bags instead of one when you start out for your new case," Vail had said. "I'm not very strong on sending you out on it, but you know how long a rope old Judge Parker can swing in Washington."

Longarm was no stranger to Judge Isaac Parker, the "Hanging Judge" of the Western Arkansas Judicial District in Little Rock. He said, "You mean he's wanting me to pull his men's chestnuts out of the fire again, Billy? It wasn't too long ago that we helped him out. Seems to me it's getting to be a habit."

"I think he's got a pretty good reason this time," Vail replied.

"Sure. He's real good at coming up with reasons."

"This case involves some Indian agents," Vail went on. "And they're sure to know all of Judge Parker's men by sight. He needs a face they won't recognize off-hand."

"More crookedness in the Indian Bureau?"

"Something like that," the chief marshal said nodding. "You know what a mess of thieves that outfit is, anyhow. They steal from the government and they steal from the factoring outfits that supply the reservations and they steal from the redskins, so it doesn't surprise me a bit that now they're starting to steal from each other."

"And this stealing's all going on in Judge Parker's

jurisdiction?" Longarm frowned. "I thought his district stopped at the Indian Nation's borders."

"You've dealt with the judge more than once," Vail said. "You should've learned by now that he doesn't pay a bit of mind to lines on a map."

"I ought to have figured that out myself," Longarm said. "I guess I just didn't remember."

Vail went on "The long and the short of it is that some young Cherokee squaw who works for the Indian Agency tumbled onto what was going on and didn't know anybody but Judge Parker that she could take her story to. She was afraid that some of the tribe's elders might be mixed up in the mess."

"So she went to Judge Parker, and he just took over from there, I guess."

"Something like that. Anyhow, the judge wants a man from outside that area to close up the case, and what Judge Parker wants, he generally gets."

"And he picked me out, did he?"

"First name out of the hat." Vail nodded. "But if it'll make you feel any better, you don't have to get involved in the case except to make the arrests. This Cherokee squaw did all the spying that was needed, so she'll be the one who has to testify when the crooks come to trial. All you'll have to do is go to Tahlequah—that's the Cherokee capital, or whatever they call it—and wait until those thieving Indian agents meet to split up their loot. You arrest them, take them to Fort Smith and deliver them to the judge, then get on the next train home. Here."

"You sure make it sound easy, Billy."

"Well, dammit, Long! It is easy! You don't have to

4

lift a finger except to put the handcuffs on a bunch of thieves."

"Now, Billy, I've heard you say that before about a case, and before I've closed it up I've lost a week's sleep and been chased all around hell's half-acre and been shot at by God knows how many outlaws."

"I'll admit that things don't always work out the way they look to from the start," Vail agreed. "But I don't see that there's much chance of it happening this time."

"How many in the bunch I'll be after?" Longarm asked.

"Three or four. They're not really certain yet how many of the Indian Agency men are tied together in it."

"Well, it sure don't sound like much of a job, Billy. I might as well be doing it as cooling my heels here, waiting for you to send me someplace else. When do you want me to leave?"

"Tomorrow's as good a day as any. You might have to wait a day or so after you get there, but from what Judge Parker said in his telegram, the crooks are going to get together and split up their loot sometime within the next week."

"How come they're taking so long to divvy up?"

"One of them—the boss of the bunch, I understand—had to go to Washington to settle up some kind of squabble. He'll be back by the time you get there, though."

"Well, if that's the way it is, I guess I better get ready and leave," Longarm said. He stood up and stretched. "Henry will have all my travel vouchers and stuff ready for me to leave tomorrow, I guess?"

"They'll be ready before the day's out."

"I'll be on the morning eastbound flyer, then." Longarm nodded. "And I don't reckon you've got anything for me to do the rest of the day, so I'll sashay over to my room and pack."

Now, following Relimee through the heavy underbrush of the broad river-bottom, Longarm could see the end of his case drawing close. Relimee had been expecting him when he arrived in Tahlequah two days earlier. Following the instructions that had been sent by Judge Parker, Longarm had neither identified himself as a deputy U.S. marshal, nor asked for Relimee by name when he went into the busy Indian Bureau office in the Cherokee Nation's capital.

Instead, he'd brought out one of his faithful ruses. It was the trick he used when trying to locate someone he didn't know, inventing a name and asking a stranger the whereabouts of the nonexistent individual, and hoping while he waited for a reply that he hadn't inadvertently used the name of a real person. When a young woman came up to the reception counter in the Indian Bureau office in Tahlequah and he'd asked for the fictitious person he'd just invented, she'd shaken her head as she frowned and studied Longarm's face.

"I'm afraid there isn't anyone by that name in Tahlequah," she'd told him. "But you might ask at the tribal newspaper just down the street. The man you're looking for might not be on our office roll, he may have just married one of our women, and in that case all that would be on our roster is her Cherokee name."

Before Longarm could reach the newspaper office, Relimee had overtaken him. "I hope you're the United States marshal I've been expecting," she gasped, a bit breathless after hurrying to catch up. "Judge Parker

6

wrote me that you'd be getting here and gave me a little description of you."

"My name's Long, ma'am," Longarm replied. "Custis Long. And I reckon I'm the one you're expecting. I just took the chance you were the lady I was looking for, after I'd looked around for a minute. I figured you wouldn't want anybody knowing who I was really looking for, so I made up a name to use."

"That was quick thinking, Marshal Long," Relimee said. "I'm Relimee Bates. You were right, I didn't want anybody in the bureau office to know I was meeting a United States marshal."

"Is there someplace close by where we can go talk a minute or two?" he asked. "It might not be a good idea for somebody to see you and me together, even out here on the street."

"It isn't. Like all towns, Tahlequah's full of gossips. We can't talk here on the street, and I can't risk being away from the office more than a minute or two. Suppose we meet after supper, just before dark. The capitol building's right across the street from the newspaper office, and it's as good a place as any. I'll be there at dusk."

While he and Relimee talked the evening before, walking along the side streets of Tahlequah, Longarm had learned for the first time the details of the crooked Indian agents' activities. The swindlers had reaped a rich harvest by stealing from the tribal allotment payments that were still being made by the U.S. Indian Agency to the Cherokees.

Brennan and his accomplices had used a very simple device in their thievery. The allotment payments arrived

7

each month from Washington, a bulk sum totaling tens of thousands of dollars, transferred by a draft on the U.S. Treasury. The agents were then supposed to convert the draft to cash at the federal bank in Little Rock, and apportion out the money to the individual members of the Cherokee tribe who'd been forced to abandon their homes and farms on the eastern seaboard and resettle in Indian Territory, almost a thousand miles to the west.

Although the long march—which the Indians called the Trail of Tears—had been made almost a half century earlier, the memory of its hardships remained fresh, kept alive by the tribe's elders, most of whom had been children at the time. Congress had finally recognized its injustice, and made cash allotments to the tribe—not as a tribe, but as individuals.

By pocketing part of the allotment payments from some of the tribesmen, and by padding the tribal roster with false names, the crooked Indian agents were stealing government money at the rate of more than twenty thousand dollars per month. When Relimee had finished telling Longarm of the extent and duration of the thefts by the small group of Indian agents, Longarm had whistled softly.

"Why, those crooks are getting rich!" he exclaimed.

"Yes, I know," the Cherokee girl replied. "And from money that rightfully belongs to our people. I'm sure I don't have to tell you that they won't stop at murder to keep their secrets."

"How many you figure are going to be at this meeting when they split their loot?"

"At least five. There's a place in the Arkansas River bottoms where they'll get together. It's rough country, so if you'd like for me to get some of the men of our people to go with us tomorrow night—"

"No need," Longarm broke in. "From what my chief told me, Judge Parker wants to keep this quiet. Seems there are a few of the gang that he's still got to have his deputy marshals round up."

"We'll go alone then?"

"Not we, ma'am. Me."

"Marshal Long, you'll never find your way alone to the place they'll be meeting," Relimee argued. "It took me three days to locate the little hut they use. I'll have to go with you if you expect to capture them."

"Oh, I aim to take 'em in all right," Longarm said. He did not speak boastfully, just stated his intention as a fact.

"Then you'll need me to guide you to the place," Relimee said firmly. "I have enough sense not to get in your way. Now, we can either go early to be at that little hut before dark, so you can look at the hut and the area around it, or we can get to it after dark, when all of those agents are inside, dividing up their loot. Which do you think is better?"

Longarm had encountered enough willful women in the past to know when he was talking to one who meant what she said. He'd also learned from past experience that Cherokee women were not at all awed by the men of the tribe, but stood with them on an equal plane. He did not acknowledge the minor defeat he'd just experienced, though.

"Right after dark, I'd say," he replied.

"Then we'll leave here about four o'clock," Relimee said. "That'll get us to the hut were they're meeting about a half hour after sunset."

• • •

9

Longarm and Relimee had left Tahlequah as planned, riding for the most part on an old trail that led along the winding and zigzagging course of the Little Illinois River. There'd been a half dozen fords to splash across as they rode south, and just before sunset they'd reached the mouth of the stream, where it flowed along a huge triangular sand spit for almost two miles before emptying into the bigger waters of the Arkansas River.

"Their shack's just about a half mile from the high-water mark on that spit of land," Relimee had told him, pointing along the riverbank to a broad, jutting sand spit thinly covered with scrub brush. "If you—" She broke off as a rider came into sight. He was riding toward the area to which she'd just pointed. She went on, saying, "We're here too early, I'm afraid. That man's my boss, Gil Brennan. And if he looks this way, we're close enough for him to see me and recognize me!"

Longarm wasted no time in argument. He grabbed the reins of Relimee's horse, wheeled his own mount by heeling it, and led the way back toward the thicker growth of bushes and scrub live-oaks that filled the area through which they'd just passed.

As quickly as he'd moved, their retreat had started too late. Before they could reach cover, a rifle cracked behind them and hot lead spurted from the yellow soil between their horses.

Twisting in his saddle, he whipped his Winchester out of its saddle scabbard and triggered off two quick unaimed shots at their attacker. Even at such close range his snapshots missed. Both slugs raised spurts of sand short of the crooked Indian agent, but they'd served their purpose by forcing Brennan to crouch down on his horse's back instead of getting off an aimed shot that might have been more deadly than his first two.

During the few moments taken up by the exchange of rifle fire, Relimee's horse had come up until she and Longarm were sitting knee to knee on their mounts. She pointed to the thicket beyond the scrub growth from which they'd just emerged.

"If we can get to it, that brush will hide us," she said.

Longarm had already reached the same conclusion. He let go of her mount's saddle and said, "Let's make it, then!"

Galloping stirrup-to-stirrup, they raced across the sandy soil and into the thin scrub. Behind them they could hear Gil Brennan's shouts, and in the few minutes that passed before they could plunge into the thicker brush that covered the widening tongue of land, they heard the fainter shouts replying to Brennan's calls.

"He must've been the last one to get to their meeting," Relimee called to Longarm as they approached the winding line where bare sand studded only here and there with short weeds gave way to a ragged line of thicker brush.

"Sure sounds like he's going to have some of his crooked pals with him," Longarm agreed. He was studying the terrain in front of them as he spoke. The country ahead gave little promise of more effective cover. Scrub river-bottom cedar, not high enough to hide a horseback rider, formed a wavering line across the sandy soil of the widening spit. "And that stuff up ahead's a mite too spotty to give us much cover."

"There's a blind canyon a little bit farther on," she told him. "If we can get to it before Brennan and his friends catch up, we can hide in it."

"Hiding from trouble never did cure it," Longarm

replied. A shot rang out from their pursuers as he spoke, but the man firing was far off target. The slug whistled through the still air fifty or sixty feet away from them. Longarm went on, "We got to get to cover soon as we can, or they'll be able to cut us down."

"Then the canyon's our best bet," Relimee said.

"I reckon so. If we can stretch things out, maybe they'll figure that we've run away and go on with their scheme to split up their loot."

"It wouldn't surprise me," she agreed. "They've gotten away with so much so easily that they're as likely to go through with their plans as they'd be to give them up for now."

"You're sure you know where this canyon opens up?"

"Of course I am, Marshal Long! I grew up on this part of the reservation. As youngsters we used to play hide and seek in the canyon, even though our parents had ordered us to stay away from it. They called it the Devil's Split, but that didn't keep us away from it. The mouth's closer to the river than we are now, so if we're going to take cover in it we'd better start veering to our left."

"You take the lead, then," Longarm told her. As he spoke he was putting fresh shells into the Winchester's magazine, replacing the rounds he'd fired. "I'll keep the varmints from getting too close to us."

Relimee nodded and reined her horse on a slant toward the straggling line of cedars. Longarm looked back at the men who were pursuing them. The distance between them was still great enough to give him some encouragement, but he could see at once that shooting from the saddle at distant targets was not going to be a practical matter. He reined in and turned his horse in order to be facing their pursuers. They were still scattered in a ragged line of three, but they'd gained no ground on him and Relimee as yet.

Knowing that the horses would be better targets than their riders, who were bending low in their saddles as they rode, Longarm stood up in his stirrups. Taking as careful aim as was possible while holding his balance on the restless horse, he triggered off three shots in quick succession, shooting low, at the horses rather than the men.

His aim was better than he'd thought it could be under the circumstances. The horse ridden by one of the crooked agents broke stride and stumbled. It did not go down, but the man in its saddle was obviously fighting the reins, swaying from side to side to keep his balance as the animal veered in its broken gait. Longarm snapped off another quick shot, and this time he aimed for the rider.

A yell of pain reached him faintly as the Indian agent at whom he'd aimed dropped his reins and folded his arms over his chest. Bullets were pocking the ground uncomfortably close to Longarm now as the other two agents turned their rifles on him. The man on the wounded horse was shouting now. Longarm could not make out his words, but there was no need for him to overhear what the man was saying. The other two had abandoned their attack and were already reining in their companion's direction.

For a split second Longarm debated riding back to shoot from closer range, but the men who were riding to join the one on the wounded horse saw him halting and began shooting again.

Hot lead cut the air on both sides of Longarm's exposed position. He saw that he had no real alternative, turned his mount, spurred ahead, and in a few minutes had caught up with Relimee. She was turning to look back at him, and when she saw him approaching she nodded in the direction she was taking, away from the river, to a rock outcrop that rose from the sandy soil a hundred or so yards ahead. It was not until Longarm got within speaking distance that he saw the bloodstain on the upper arm of her blouse.

"You got hit!" he exclaimed.

"Yes. A wild shot. But it's only a graze. It won't bother me a bit." Relimee nodded toward the low ledges of eroding rock ahead of them. "The mouth of the canyon's right up ahead. What are the agents doing?"

"I nicked one of their horses. The others went to help him."

"If we hurry we can get to the canyon before they see us again," she said. "Don't worry about my arm. I've been hurt worse when my skinning knife slipped while I was helping my mother butcher out a steer."

Relimee dug her heels into her horse's flanks and headed for the jagged stone formation which was now only a hundred yards away from them. Longarm followed her after a quick look back. He could catch a glimpse of the outlaw agents through the scrub, but could not see the men clearly enough to tell what they were doing. Reining around, he followed the Cherokee girl toward the rock outcrop.

# Chapter 2

When Relimee was within a dozen yards of the low, striated face of the stone ledge, she turned her horse and rode along its base, heading now toward the river. Longarm followed her without hesitation. He twisted in his saddle occasionally to look back, for he was sure the two renegade Indian agents remaining would not stay surprised very long.

They could hear the gurgling current of the river ahead of them when their pursuers came into sight again. They agents had apparently left the body of their companion after they'd gotten over their surprise and were galloping after them. Longarm caught little more than a glimpse of their faces before the men were hidden by the curve of the high stone bluff.

"Have we got much farther to go?" he called to Relimee.

"Just a little way," she replied, looking over her shoulder at him. "The canyon's mouth is only about fifty or sixty feet ahead."

"Looks like we'll make it inside before they can see us, then," Longarm told her. "I sure hope that place is wide enough for us to ride into."

"It's been a long time since I was at the canyon," Relimee said. "And the entrance isn't very easy to see. But unless I've forgotten something about this place, we're almost there now."

Longarm looked ahead. All that he could see was the curved face of the bluff they were following. Behind them he could hear the gurgling flow of the river, but the stream itself was invisible. He said nothing more, and in a few minutes Relimee slowed her horse to a walk and pointed ahead.

"There's a gap in the cliff face a little bit farther along, and we'll turn into it," she told him. "The canyon is oh, maybe a hundred feet up a little slope. I haven't been near it for a long time, but if I remember correctly we can squeeze the horses inside with us. If we can't, we'll just have to leave them outside and hope that our luck holds good."

Only a few moments after she'd finished speaking, Relimee reined her horse into a narrow slit in the sheer stone wall. Longarm followed her into the cramped opening that broke the rock face. It was less a canyon than a split in the massive rock formation. There was room for them to ride their horses into it, but after they'd ridden between the sheer, towering walls for twenty or thirty yards the crevice narrowed sharply.

Ahead, Longarm noticed that the cleft in the stone extended fewer than a dozen paces beyond the point where Relimee had reined in. He glanced around, but saw no sign of an opening in its sheer, high walls. Relimee had started to dismount. Longarm followed suit, and walked over to where she was standing beside her pony.

"If you're looking for the entrance to the canyon, it's not all that easy to see," she told him. "It's a few steps farther along, and I'm still not sure that we'll be able to get the horses into it with us." As she spoke, she was looking down at the bloodstain on the left sleeve of her blouse.

"How bad are you hurt?" Longarm asked.

"It stings a bit. But it's only a little scratch."

"I'll look at it after we're safe, then."

With a nod Relimee started toward the end of the blind canyon. Longarm followed her. They'd taken only a half dozen steps before the black opening of the canyon showed in the sheer wall to their left. It was a narrow triangle, only a little wider at the bottom than at the top, and Longarm could see at a glance that getting the horses into it would be something of a squeeze.

"What do you think?" Relimee asked.

"I think we better see if we can get the nags inside with us. There sure ain't no other place to hide them if your friends out there stumble onto this canyon. But first we better look and see what it's like inside, unless you remember some more about it from when you used to play in it."

"I'm sorry, Marshal Long, but it's been a long time, and I was just a little girl looking for a place to play. It seems a lot smaller now than it did to me then, though."

"Sure. Except it's the other way around. You were a lot littler then."

"I suppose that's right."

"We might have to keep watch at the mouth and fight them off from there," Longarm said.

"That would be a better plan, if only I had a rifle," she said. "But since I don't . . ."

Longarm nodded and said, "Sure. We'll have to look and see how the land lays before we decide what's the best thing to do."

They stepped cautiously into the cleft. Underfoot, the floor was soft, yielding sand. For a moment their bodies blocked off its opening, and Longarm wondered what they would do next if it proved too narrow to admit the horses and hide them. Then they'd passed the slit and were inside. The waning light of the long sunset after-

17

glow showed that within a few feet past its slitlike mouth the canyon widened appreciably.

"It'll be a tight squeeze getting the horses in, but maybe we can coax 'em," Longarm said thoughtfully. He lifted his arms, measuring the distance between the walls. When he found that he could touch both sides with flattened palms, he asked, "Does it widen out any more, up ahead?"

"As I remember, it does. But not a lot, not until you've gone twenty or thirty feet. I never did go very far from where we are now."

"We won't know till we try," Longarm told her. "Suppose you stay inside here. I'll go see if I can push the horses in through the opening."

Getting the horses through the small passage was a job, but not one as hard as they'd imagined it might be. Once the animals had been persuaded to stick their heads into the slit's opening, and Relimee could take hold of their bridles, the animals moved readily enough, though their flanks scraped against the stone walls now and then. By the time both horses had been led inside and past the squeeze of the narrow opening gap, the animals were moving readily. When they reached the point where the cavern widened, they stood quietly.

"We got some catching up to do real quick," Longarm told Relimee. "You've worked for the Indian Agency, so I reckon you know who that fellow was that I dropped."

"That was Nathan Luther. He's the one that's in charge of the Shawnees and Senecas and Delawares on the reservation just to the north of the Cherokee lands."

"And in this robbing scheme up to his neck like the others, I guess?"

"Of course. One of the others is Gil Brennan. He's

the one I work for at the Cherokee Agency. And the third man is Tom Ames. He's the supervisor."

"You mean the boss of all the other agents?"

"Yes. I don't see him very often, but I'm sure about who he is."

"This is a bigger scheme than I figured." Longarm frowned. "No wonder they're dead set on getting rid of you."

"That's why I had to go to Judge Parker," Relimee said. "He was the only one I could think of that I could trust."

"Well, you sure did the right thing," Longarm assured her. "But instead of us going on talking right now, I oughta be taking a look at that bullet wound you got. It'll have to be bandaged up."

"It's nothing," Relimee assured him. "Just a graze. It's already stopped bleeding."

"Well, if you're sure you're all right, suppose you stay here with the nags and keep 'em from getting feisty," Longarm told Relimee. The sky overhead was darkening now, and gave them the feeling that they were totally cut off from the world. By the fading light that still trickled into the canyon Longarm could see Relimee only as a vague form outlined against the animals. "I'll go back and take a look-see. We better be sure what them fellows outside are up to now."

She nodded, and Longarm slid his rifle from its saddle scabbard before starting back toward the mouth of the cleft. He groped along the wall to the ledge and stepped out onto it. From that height he could get a glimpse of the river, a streak of greenish water burbling between steep banks. As he moved he noticed that the daylight was slowly fading. The sky had not yet darkened, but its blue was deeper now than it had been even the few minutes past when they'd entered the cave, a sign that the sun had now dipped below the horizon.

His rifle ready, he stepped outside and stood listening. Above the steep wall behind him the sky was slowly deepening into the long twilight that would hold the arid land before full night arrived, and except for the faint whispering of the river, the evening was quiet. He was getting ready to return to the cave when Brennan's voice broke the silence. Longarm stopped in his tracks. The men's voices were so loud in the stillness that he was sure they were close enough to see him even in the failing light.

"Any sign of 'em over there where you are, Tom?" Brennan called.

"Not hair nor hide!" Ames shouted back.

"I don't guess they got close enough to get a good look at us," Brennan went on. "But I've seen the woman too many times to be mistaken, even if I just got one quick look at her. She's that Cherokee squaw, Relimee, that works for me."

"Now, that's a hell of a note!" Tom Ames exclaimed. "What's she doing here? I thought she was supposed to be working at her job back at Tahlequah."

"That's the mistake I made!" Brennan answered angrily. "And I don't know the answer yet, but I'll correct it quick when we catch up to her and whoever it is with her. It's a hell of a note when you can't trust nobody anymore!"

"Well, we're not far from the river now," Ames said. "There's just a little narrow strip of sand between the water and this big cliff. If they intend to try getting away by riding along the bank, we'll see 'em for sure even if it is getting dark real fast."

"Keep an eye on the river, too," Brennan warned.

"They might be trying to swim their horses across. But if that's what they aim to do, they'll be sitting ducks. Dark or no dark, we could spot 'em in easy in the water."

"That's right," Ames agreed. "We'll just knock them off their horses and let 'em float downstream. Nobody's likely to think they ever were anyplace near here. They'll figure they got killed close to one of the towns farther up the river, Enfaula or Checota or someplace like that."

By this time the two agents were riding past the cleft where Longarm was hidden, watching them. He pressed as flat as he could make himself against the wall of the cliff and froze. The two men were opposite the opening. Both carried rifles, and Longarm knew without any speculation that they were more than ready to use their weapons.

Brennan and Tom Ames were watching the area in front of them, and on horseback their heads were just a few inches below Longarm's boot soles. If it had not been for the rattlesnake on the narrow trail they followed, they would have gone by without noticing him.

Longarm himself did not see the rattler until Brennan's horse shied and reared up on its hind legs. The Indian agent yelled as the horse snorted, but his surprise did not show in his quick reaction as he lowered the muzzle of his rifle to shoot the snake. The rifle barked and Tom brought up his own weapon.

"What the hell!" he shouted.

"Snake!" Brennan yelled. Both riders had reined in now. Brennan added, "Rattler! It damn near struck my nag in the leg! Would've, if I hadn't've shot it."

"Well, you sure took me by surprise," Ames said. He lifted his wide-brimmed hat and reached into his hip pocket for his bandanna. It was a wad in his hand and he shook it to unfold it, his eyes automatically turning toward the fluttering kerchief. It was then that he saw Longarm's boots on the ledge above Brennan's head.

"Look out, Gil!" he yelled, letting his bandanna drop to the ground and bringing up his rifle to fire. "They're right up over your head on a ledge!"

Longarm dropped flat as he saw Ames's rifle muzzle covering him. The rifle spat as he hit the ground, the slug glancing off the stone wall behind him. Lying prone, hugging the rock ledge, he found that he could no longer see either of the crooked Indian agents. He was as invisible to them as they were to him, and he had no intention of wasting his scarce supply of ammunition by shooting at invisible targets.

Longarm began crawfishing backward, propelling himself by his knees and boot toes. He kept his eyes on the edge of the ledge, ready to shoot if either of his enemies raised his head above it. He'd almost reached the break that led to the canyon's mouth when he heard stones rattling against the wall of the cliff, and in a moment the crown of the light-colored Stetson that he remembered seeing on Ames's head broke the jagged line of the rim. For a moment Longarm held his fire, then the hat began to rise again, like a ghost in the gathering darkness. He triggered off a shot. The Stetson flew through the air like a bird, uncovering the rifle barrel that Ames had been using to lift it. The rifle was lowered quickly. The the Indian agent's voice came drifting over the rim.

"Whoever that fellow is, he's a good shot. If we're going to get rid of him and the girl, we'll have to move careful."

"Maybe we'd better wait for Soames and Warren to

get here," Brennan suggested. "One on one's not very good odds in my book. Four on two sure would be a hell of a lot better than what we've got now."

"It's your call, Gil," Ames said. "You're responsible for all this. That damned squaw works for you, and she never should've found out about our scheme. But we'll talk about that later. Right now we've got to take care of those two up on the ledge. It's up to us to be damn sure they don't get away."

"I say we wait, then," Brennan went on. "I don't know what's holding up Soames and Warren, they're way overdue. But as soon as they get here we can put them on the cliff up above that ledge and close in on that cut they've holed up in."

"How're Soames and Warren going to know where we are? They might be waiting for us now, back at the shanty."

"I was getting to that," Brennan said. "I'll go back and see if they're there yet. If they're not, I'll wait until they show up, and all three of us will come on back. All you have to do is keep those two holed up until we get here. They're likely to try and make a getaway, now that it's dark."

Longarm decided he'd heard enough. He sidled back along the ledge. Relimee was standing just outside the canyon's narrow, high mouth.

"I could hear their voices, but couldn't make out what they were saying," she told him. "I guess you could, though."

"Plain enough. They're going to wait till their friends get here, two fellows. One's named Soames, the other one's Warren. They they're figuring to come after us. But we got a little time now to do some moving of our own."

23

"What do you mean?" she asked.

"I mean we better move pretty quick, if they're looking for some more to get here. You'd know who they are, I guess?"

"Soames is in charge of the biggest reservation in the Indian Nation. It cuts right through the middle, and there're a dozen tribes who have their land on it. Warren's responsible for the Comanche land, farther west."

"I'll say this for you, Relimee, you sure tore down a lot of playhouses for that ring of crooks," Longarm told her. "But we better not waste any more time. There's not but one man down there on guard now, and being dark outside gives us a better chance, too."

"I was thinking the same thing," she said. "All we'll need is a little bit of a start, and he won't be able to see us. When, Longarm?"

"We'll wait a minute, till this one down below gets over being restless and the other one's too far away to do anything even if he hears shooting, then we'll give it a try."

"What about the horses?"

"It's too big of a job to squeeze 'em out of that narrow place when it's pitch-black like this. They'll just have to stay here till daylight. We won't be going very far. My job's to bring these fellows in, and that's what I aim to do."

"You mean you're going to try to capture all of them?" Relimee asked him. "What about the two that haven't showed up yet? And Gil Brennan? He's going to bring them with him when he comes back."

"Oh, I ain't forgetting about Brennan and the other two. But let's corral that one down below first. Then we'll worry about the others. You just hunker down here. I'm going—" Longarm broke off as a thin wisp of

24

smoke rose above the edge of the ledge in front of the canyon. The wisp grew steadily larger.

"Ames certainly isn't planning to move, or he wouldn't have lighted a fire," Relimee said. "Maybe he did it to guide the ones who're coming back."

"That's likely," Longarm replied. "But we won't wait for them to get here. Now that I know who he is, I have to do something I hadn't been figuring on."

"What's that?"

"I have to give him a chance to surrender peaceful."

"You're joking!" she gasped. "After what he's done? Not just robbing the Indians he was supposed to protect, but shooting at us and chasing us and all!"

Longarm shook his head. "No, Relimee. I ain't joshing you one bit. He's a sorta high-up muckety-muck in that damn Indian Bureau, which makes his boss the same as mine."

"I guess I don't understand," she said.

"It's simple as one–two–three," Longarm told her. "A while ago, when he and the other crooks were after us, they shot first, so I had all the right in the world to shoot back. But now I know who Ames is. If I just throw down on him and shoot him, even if I give him a fair chance in a face-off, there's going to be a lot of hollering between the high-muckety-mucks in the Justice Department and in the Indian Bureau."

"And you'll be caught up in the middle."

"Not just me, but my chief in Denver, Billy Vail. So all I can do this time is follow rules." Raising his voice, Longarm called, "Tom Ames! Are you listening to me down there?"

A long silence followed. Then Ames called back, "I'm listening, but before I say anything more I want to know who I'm listening to."

25

"My name's Long, Ames," Longarm replied. "Deputy U.S. marshal out of the Denver office. I'm putting you and your men under arrest and asking you to surrender peaceful."

There was another silence, but it was shorter than the first one. Then Ames asked, "You'd be the one they call Longarm, I suppose?"

"Folks tag me that way sometimes," Longarm agreed.

"I hear you like to shoot first and ask questions later," Ames said. "Make yourself the judge and jury and hangman all at the same time."

"What you've heard and what the truth is are two different stories," Longarm replied calmly. He understood the Indian agent's purpose in making the taunting remark. Ames was trying to anger him, get him off balance, to gain an advantage for himself. The trick had been tried on Longarm too many times in the past to have any effect on him. He went on, "Now, I'm coming down there to put the handcuffs on you. If you're smart as I figure you to be, you'll lay your gun down and surrender."

This time Ames answered at once. His voice was hard as he called, "Surrender, hell, Long! I'm not giving up to you! If you think you're going to arrest me, you'll have to come down here and get me!"

Longarm had anticipated the Indian agent's reply. He'd put his Winchester down at Relimee's feet, and moved almost before the crooked Indian agent's words left his mouth. Bending double, he ran back along the narrow ledge for a half dozen long, leaping steps, then leapt from the ledge down to the soft sandy soil that extended inland to the escarpment from the riverbank.

Landing on his feet in the yielding sand, Longarm

lurched forward the step or two needed to hold his balance, then turned and moved back to the face of the bluff that rose sheer above him. Pressing against the curving stone formation, he began sidling slowly in the direction of the river. He kept his eyes moving over the barren, river-scoured stretch of sand that ran from the base of the cliff down to the water's edge. No sign of movement was visible anywhere.

Gauging his position as best he could by the distance from the stream to the base of the stone bluff, Longarm inched along. He'd covered a dozen feet when he saw Ames's horse. It stood between the face of the bluff and the steep dip that ran to the edge of the river. The bulge of the barren sandbank between the base of the cliff and the stream hid the water, though even in the fast-fading light he could get a glimpse or two of its roiled surface where the bank dipped.

When Ames's gun barked, it was from the direction Longarm had least expected, the riverbank. He got a fleeting glimpse of the crooked Indian agent as Ames raised up behind the steeply slanting sands to snapshot a slug from his rifle before dropping back below the sandbank. His bullet fell short, the common mistake of a man unaccustomed to aiming uphill. Ames's lead kicked up the surface of the riverbank a yard short of Longarm's boot toes.

Longarm did not reply with a shot of his own. Instead he dropped flat, his face to the sand, his arms outstretched above his head, his Colt grasped in his right hand. He'd been careful to fall with his face to the right, and between his slitted eyelids he could scan the riverbank for several yards in each direction. A minute ticked off, then another. With the patience that was ingrained after so many years as a lawman, Longarm waited.

Ames showed himself at last. Longarm glimpsed him rising, a dark silhouette against the last vestiges of the waning twilight. It was the moment he'd been waiting for. He did not rise or move his shoulders. Raising his gun hand he triggered off a shot from his Colt. The slug went true. Ames staggered erect for a fleeting fraction of a second, then crumpled into a heap of lifeless flesh on the sandbank which had been his shelter.

After the echoes of Longarm's Colt died away, Relimee called from the ledge, "Longarm! Are you all right?"

"I'm fine," he replied. He paused long enough to light the thin cigar he'd slid from his pocket, then went on, "And Ames isn't going to bother us anymore. But you better come on down now, Relimee. We have to get ready for the others. They'll be getting here pretty soon, if Brennan's found 'em like he was supposed to. And I have a pretty good notion of how we can take 'em."

# Chapter 3

"How in the world can you hope to get all three of those men to surrender?" Relimee asked.

"A scheme popped into my mind a little bit ago," Longarm replied. "Maybe it won't work worth a damn, but it'll sure save us a lot of trouble if it does."

"I'd like to hear about it."

"Oh, I'm getting ready to tell you, Relimee. You've been such a big help so far that I figure we got a good chance to make it work."

"Go on," she said. "I'm ready to do almost anything that'll settle this without a gunfight."

"That's not likely," Longarm told her soberly. "Those crooked agents have got too much to lose not to fight."

"I suppose you're right. We don't have much choice, do we? Go ahead, then. Tell me what you've worked out."

"Well, to start with, you won't be doing much besides sitting still. I hope you won't get upset if I ask you to put on a dead man's coat. You'll need to wear the one that Ames has got on, if it's not too bloody and torn up."

"You mean that I'm going to be posing as Tom Ames?"

"That's the general idea." Longarm nodded.

"Do you really think those Indian agents will be fooled?" Relimee frowned. "Why, they see him every month or so, so they'll know right away that I'm not him."

"Not in the dark, Relimee. You see, they'll be looking into the firelight with you in-between. All you'll look like is a black blob. It came to me when I saw Ames outlined against the sky a minute or so ago, after he popped up outa no place to shoot me. With the light behind his face he could've been just about anybody."

"Suppose they do recognize me, though, and see that I'm not Ames?"

"Don't worry. I'll be ready if that happens."

"You won't be with me by the fire, then?"

Longarm shook his head. "I'll be off in the dark, where they won't see me. But they won't have much time to study you, because by the time they're stepping up to the fire, I'll have 'em covered from behind."

Relimee was silent for a moment, then she nodded slowly. "You know, Longarm, even if it did sound like it was a crazy scheme when you started telling me about it, your plan just might work. I'm ready to try it, anyhow."

"Then let's go down to the river. It's not too dark yet for us to see, so we oughta be able to pick up enough driftwood along the bank to build up the fire Ames started. And I'll stop long enough to take Ames's coat off him and pick up his hat. I reckon you can wrap your skirt around your legs enough so they'll look like you've got on a pair of pants."

In spite of the darkness, the river's surface still reflected what brightness remained in the after-sunset sky. They had to spend only a few minutes exploring along the high-water mark in order to pick up enough dry driftwood to help the small fire. While Relimee carried the wood back to the base of the cliff, Longarm took on the unpleasant job of removing the dead man's coat and picking up his hat and rifle. He rolled Ames's lifeless body the few feet necessary to hide it behind one of the

30

high spots of the riverbank, then carried the coat and hat back to the small fire which Relimee was kindling.

"Soon as you slip on this coat and hat, take this rifle and get hunkered down by the fire. I'll keep the pistol. Then I'll go find a good place where I can wait for Brennan and them other fellows," Longarm said. He handed Ames's coat and hat and rifle to Relimee. "There're a few spots of blood on the coat. I sure hope you don't mind."

"A little blood won't bother me," she said. "I've helped my mother and the other women clean agency steers. And I've seen a few men shot or cut up in a knife fight. One thing I've learned is that you can always wash blood away when it gets on your hands."

"How's your arm feeling now? I'm sorry we haven't had enough time to put a bandage on it."

"It doesn't bother me a bit. You saw for yourself that it was just a little scratch. It stopped bleeding almost at once. I've been hurt a lot worse being thrown off a horse."

"Well, if our luck don't run out, we'll have those crooked agents corralled and be taking 'em to Fort Smith by daybreak tomorrow," Longarm said. "You'll likely have to stay there a few days before Judge Parker has got time on his court calendar to try 'em."

"You'll be staying too, won't you? You're the one who's arresting them."

"That'll depend on what the judge wants. If Billy Vail needs me, I'll likely go right back. But that'll depend on what Judge Parker wants. About the only thing I'm sure of is that he won't go easy on 'em."

"Yes, I'm sure of that, too," she said. "It's one reason I waited to tell anybody about what I'd found out until I had a chance to go to Fort Smith and pass my

31

information on to him. He was—" Relimee broke off as the sound of hoofbeats broke the early night's stillness, then she said, "That must be Brennan and the others coming now."

"Likely it is," Longarm said. "You better hunker down. Just be sure to keep your back to 'em till I've had time to step up in behind 'em."

"I'll act like I've dozed off sitting up," she said, stepping to the edge of the fire.

Putting on the coat and hat quickly, Relimee chose a spot at the edge of the circle of dim reddish light cast by the little blaze, and sat down. She crossed her legs Indian style as she dropped to the ground. After she'd gotten comfortably settled, Longarm took a step or two away from the fire and turned to look back at her. Seeing her in silhouette against the small waning blaze, he decided that Relimee looked enough like Ames to deceive the other agents for the few moments that would be required.

"Just stay still the way you're sitting now," he told her. "Maybe let you head fall frontward a mite more. And don't make a single move till I've got 'em covered."

Longarm started for the deep shadows at the bottom of the stone cliff. He looked back once, and nodded to himself as a grim smile formed on his face. From where he stood, Relimee could very well have been Ames hunkered down and leaning on his rifle at the edge of the glow cast by the small flickering blaze. The hoofbeats had grown steadily louder and he hurried the few steps that were needed to carry him into the dense darkness at the base of the bluff. He was ready with his Colt poised when the three crooked Indian agents rode into the circle of firelight.

32

"Well, Soames and Warren finally got here," Brennan called as he and his companions reined up and dismounted. "They—" He stopped, and the timbre of his voice changed. "Tom?" he went on, raising his voice, "Wake up! We're all here now, let's get started and take care of those two. We'll have to finish 'em off as fast as we can."

"Talk louder, Gil," one of the other agents suggested when Relimee did not move. "Old Tom's sleeping like he was dead."

"Which he is, as a matter of fact," Longarm said quietly as he stepped out of the blackness behind the agents and into the dim light cast by the flickering fire. His Colt was leveled in his hand, its muzzle describing a short arc that covered the three agents, "Now, just stand quiet and don't make no nervous moves."

"Who in hell are you?" Brennan demanded.

"My name's Custis Long, and I'm a deputy U.S. marshal outa the Denver office. And you men are all under arrest."

"Hold on, now!" Brennan protested. "We're all Indian Bureau agents! This is an Indian reservation and we're here on official business. You don't have any right to arrest us!"

"That's either a lie or a bluff, and you know it!" Longarm said quickly. "I can arrest just about anybody except the President of the United States or a congressman while he's on government business. Now, before I run out of patience, you men just stand quiet and keep your hands still."

"You'll pay for this!" one of the other Indian agents blustered. "I've got friends in high places! Just wait until they hear about what you're trying to pull!"

"You can tell anybody anything you want to later

on," Longarm said levelly. "But the main man you'll be talking to is Judge Isaac Parker, when I hand you over to him at Fort Smith." He raised his voice slightly and went on, "All right, Relimee, you can come tie these fellows' hands now."

As Relimee got up and dropped her disguise, the Indian agents broke out into an angry gabble in spite of Longarm's warning. It was Gil Brennan who stopped them.

Raising his voice to override the other two, he said, "I think we'd all be better off if we do what the marshal says and keep quiet." There was a mixture of resignation and disgust in his tone as he went on. "If you fellows haven't heard about Marshal Long before, I have, and I'd advise you not to mess around with him. He's the one they call Longarm."

"I sure got to hand it to you, Relimee," Longarm told her as they sat after a late supper in the hotel dining room. "It's just like Judge Parker said when we stopped in at his office. You've saved your people a lot of money and grief by stopping that bunch of crooked Indian agents stealing the way they were."

"You did the real work." Relimee smiled. "Or maybe we just hit it off together and that made everything come out all right."

"Well, between us, we did the job. That's all that means anything," Longarm said. "And now that it's finished, I'll ride up to Tahlequah with you and see that you get home safe and sound. Them three Indian agents we handed over to the judge might not've been the only ones that were tied in with Gil Brennan and his crooked friends."

"And from Tahlequah, you'll be going on back to Denver, I suppose?"

"Sure. I imagine by the time I get back, Billy Vail will have a new case to put me on. But that's about—" Longarm broke off as he caught sight of a familiar face, one of Judge Isaac Parker's courtroom deputies, who came into the dining room. He said, "Looks like we might have some company. That's one of Judge Parker's men, and he just might be looking for us."

By now the deputy had spotted Longarm and Relimee and was heading for their table. He reached it and said, "I had a notion this was where you and Miss Relimee would be, Longarm. Judge Parker thought he'd better have me bring this telegram to you right away, since you told him you're planning to leave early tomorrow."

As he spoke, the deputy was taking a manila-buff envelope from his pocket. He handed it to Longarm, and went on, "The judge said if you need him for anything, like lending you a horse or something of that sort, you'll know where to find him."

"Thanks," Longarm said as he took the envelope. The deputy nodded and turned to go. Longarm held the envelope in his hand, looking down at it.

"Aren't you going to open it?" Relimee asked.

"Oh, sure. But from what that deputy said about a horse, there's something tells me I ain't going to like what I got a hunch is inside of it." Longarm ripped the flap open and took out the message.

He looked at the few lines of telegrapher's Spencerian script on the sheet of flimsy and shook his head.

"Looks like we won't be riding back to Tahlequah together after all," he told Relimee.

"Let me guess," she said. "It's from your chief in

Denver. He's sending you somewhere on another case, now that your job's finished here."

"That's about the size of it," Longarm replied. "He says that seeing as I'm in the neighborhood, I might as well go on down to Texas and pick up a prisoner that's in jail there and bring him to Denver with me."

"What part of Texas?"

"Waco."

"That's a long way from Tahlequah, and in the wrong direction. I was hoping that after we got back there you might have time to spend a day or two."

Longarm shook his head. "I wish I could do that, but when Billy Vail sends me on a case, I've got no choice but to go."

"Well, riding back to Tahlequah alone doesn't bother me," Relimee said. "But I'll miss having your company, Longarm."

"Oh, that goes for me, too. I don't reckon I have to tell you that. Anyhow, seeing that both of us'll be riding out early tomorrow, I guess we better get what sleep we can."

They stood up and walked slowly through the small lobby to the stairway. Slowly, they mounted the stairs to the second-floor landing where they paused and looked at one another. Both knew that Longarm's room was on the right-hand side, Relimee's on the left.

Instead of turning away from him, Relimee tucked her hand into Longarm's elbow and said, "I don't feel like saying good night, Longarm. Or good-bye, either. How would you like to make the night last a while longer?"

Longarm was not too greatly surprised at Relimee's question. He'd encountered women from the five civilized tribes before, on other cases that had taken him to

36

the Indian Nation. Among the Cherokees and some of the other tribes, women stood equal to the men in all matters except those of hunting and fighting. They did not take the submissive secondary roles common to the warlike tribes in which the warrior was looked on as a superior being.

"I was just about to ask you if you'd like to visit with me a while," Longarm told Relimee.

"I'd about given up waiting for you to invite me," she said. "And I'm sure you know what my answer is."

Arms entwined, they walked down the corridor to Longarm's room. He unlocked the door and opened it, stood aside to let Relimee enter, then in the careful routine that had become a part of his everyday life, he closed and locked the door from the inside and hung his flat-brimmed hat on the knob where it would mask the keyhole.

Reaching into his vest pocket for a match, he drew his thumbnail across its head as he started for the small side-table where the lamp stood. Before he'd taken a second step, Relimee put out her hand and took his wrist. She pulled the burning match close to her face and blew it out.

"We don't need a light, Longarm," she said. "Half the pleasure a man and woman get when they're together for the first time is learning about each other by feeling instead of just looking."

"Whatever pleasures you, pleasures me, too," Longarm told her.

He unbuckled his gun belt, groped his way to the bed, and hung the belt over the headboard where the butt of the Colt would be within easy reach of his hand. By the time he'd shed his coat and boots and was unbuttoning his shirt his eyes had grown accustomed to the darkness. He could see Relimee as a shimmering ghostly shape, almost formless in the darkened room. The soft susurrus of cloth on skin and the movements he could make out told him that she was pulling her dress over her head.

Longarm tossed his shirt aside and pushed his balbriggans and trousers off in a single move. As he stepped aside, out of his last garments, Relimee began moving toward him. She reached his side and the delicate fragrance of freshly soap-washed woman-skin reached his nostrils.

He looked at her, his eyes straining to pierce the room's gloom, its only light now the dim glow of the hall's night-lamp that filtered in from the narrow transom above the door. Framed in the dimness he could see the white oval of Relimee's face, outlined by her long unbound hair. She stood unclothed, and he saw also the dark bosom-spots that tipped swelling breasts, and the dusky fluff of her pubic triangle, a dark patch against the creamy skin above the columns of her muscular thighs.

Then Relimee stepped up to him and brushed against him, the protruding nipples of her swelling breasts firm on his chest. Her hands ran down his sides in a rippling caress and found his burgeoning erection. She tucked the half-flaccid cylinder between her thighs and closed them tightly as her arms went around Longarm's neck, then pulled his head down until their lips met. While they prolonged their first kiss, tongues entwining, she began moving her hips back and forth very slowly, and he quickly became fully erect.

Their lips had never parted. Relimee's questing tongue was darting into Longarm's mouth each time he drew his own tongue back to breath. She was rubbing herself now against his throbbing erection, but when he reached down to place himself for a true penetration she pushed his hand aside. After what seemed a long time, Longarm wrapped his arms around Relimee and lifted her feet from the floor. He shuffled to the bed, carrying her, and lowered her gently to the mattress, still pressing to him, his erection still trapped between her thighs.

After they'd lain quietly motionless for a moment or two, Longarm raised his hips, and Relimee spread her thighs wide. He felt her hand on him, guiding him, and then was aware of the soft rasping of her dewy fuzz as she placed him. He went into her fully but gently, with a slow careful move, pressing slowly, enjoying the moist warmth as it engulfed him.

Relimee gasped and writhed as she felt him enter. She brought her legs up to lock her ankles behind his hips and began to tighten them and draw him into her more deeply. Longarm responded, but with purposeful delay. Even when Relimee tightened her leg lock he made no effort to thrust.

At last she whispered, "You're playing games with me, Longarm, and I'm ready for you to fill me! Hurry!"

Now Longarm did not wait to respond to her urging. He arched his back, then thrust hard and full, and a tiny cry of pleasure burst from Relimee's lips as she felt his swift, deep penetration. Clasping her legs around him, she lifted her hips to meet him and sighed ecstatically as she began rocking in rhythm with his long deliberate drives.

"Oh, yes!" she said into his ear. "This is what I've wanted you to do since the first time I saw you! Now I'm sorry that I waited so long. I've never found a man before who could go in this deep and fill me up the way you are!"

Longarm sought her lips with his and for the next several minutes there was silence in the room, broken only by their hoarse gasping and by the fleshy smack of their bodies each time their hips met. Longarm prolonged his steady stroking until Relimee began gasping deep in her throat, and her body took on its own rhythm in spite of her efforts to match it with Longarm's slow sustained penetrations.

"I'm building up too fast!" she gasped. "But don't slow down or stop! No matter what I say, just keep on going the way you are now!"

Longarm kept up his slow and steady rhythm while Relimee's moans and an occasional soft cry broke the room's quiet. When he felt himself building to join Relimee, he slowed down and then stopped moving except for the pressure of his body on her soft quivering form.

"What's wrong?" she whispered. "You can't stop now!"

"Just for a minute or two," he promised.

He lay motionless, still buried fully within her, and waited for Relimee's quivers to subside. Then he began stroking once more. This time he thrust faster and with greater force, still taking his time, slowing his rhythm now and again while Relimee's cries bubbled from her lips. Suddenly he felt her grow taut and then burst into a frenzy of convulsive shudders while her soft cries grew more and more urgent, and at last rose to a peak when she jerked convulsively and writhed in ecstasy beneath him.

Longarm stopped thrusting and held himself pressed firmly against her until Relimee's shuddering subsided and her cries trailed into silence. Without moving he held himself fully in her for several minutes before he started his slow deep penetrations again. Relimee accepted his drives without stirring for a short while, then her muscles began twitching and soon she was shuddering once more, her small, sharp, wordless exclamations breaking the silence of the darkened room.

Longarm was in full control of his body by now. When Relimee began writhing more vigorously and the spaces of gasping between her cries grew shorter, he increased the tempo of his strokes. He was now mounting to his own climax, ready to let nature have its way. He thrust faster and faster, and in the few moments before his body took control, Relimee's frenzied gasps poured from her lips in a single almost visible column of sound.

Then she shrieked and shuddered as Longarm drove the last deep thrusts before he began jetting. He gasped and shook while Relimee's writhings faded, and the tension drained from his own muscles as he released his control and lurched forward on her soft receptive body and lay quiet.

Neither of them stirred for several minutes. At last Relimee stirred and a long sigh of satisfaction escaped her lips. She said, "I can still feel you filling me, Longarm. Does that mean . . ."

"It means whatever you want it to."

"There's too little left of the night for us to waste any of it," she said. "I don't know how you do it, but I'm ready if you are."

She raised her hips, gently at first, then more urgently, and locked her ankles over Longarm's muscular back. He began driving again, but now he did not set the slow measured pace that marked the beginning of their first encounter. He plunged fiercely and with ever-increasing speed until Relimee tossed wildly under him

41

and her early sighs of pleasure mounted into loud cries of delight.

Longarm timed himself to meet her fast-mounting climax, and as she shuddered and moaned and locked him to her in her final writhing spasms he joined her, jetting, until he, too, was drained. Then he let himself relax on her soft quivering body until her rippling spasms faded and stopped.

Propping himself up on his elbows, he looked down at her. Relimee's long black hair was spread on the pillow, framing her face. By now their eyes had adjusted to the room's darkness, and he could see that her lips were parted in a contented smile.

"I know that I ought to be ready to sleep now," she said softly, "but I can still feel you filling me and I don't want to lose that feeling even if I do go to sleep."

"It's easy to fix that," he told her. "Just lay over on your side."

Relimee turned beneath him and Longarm let himself slump to the mattress behind her. He pressed close and Relimee needed no further hint. She moved close, pressing to him, the pair of them spooned close together.

"That's better," she said. "I can feel all of you now, and I like what I'm feeling. If I sleep a little while, will you still be here when I wake up?"

"Go ahead and nap if you want to," Longarm told her. "I'm not planning to move an inch, even if I doze off for a spell."

"I will, then," Relimee nodded. "And I'm sure you'll know just how I like to be waked up."

# Chapter 4

Longarm swung out of the caboose of the I&GN freight in the middle of the Waco yards. Dawn was still an hour away, and the night was black. He hadn't minded a bit riding with the brakemen on his trip from Fort Smith. In some ways the caboose was better than one of the dusty, green plush seats of a passengar car. Very few of Mr. Pullman's Palace Coaches were found on the new Western railroads, and the caboose of a freight train was about the only place railroads offered a bunk to a tired man who needed to catch forty winks in comfort.

Carrying his saddlebags over his shoulder and his Winchester in one hand he started along the right-of-way to the head of the train, where swinging lanterns broke the predawn gloom and he could see the forms of men beside the tracks. By the time he reached the group that seemed to be the center of activity it was breaking up, but one of the men still stood beside the tender, holding a sheaf of flimsies. Longarm recognized him as the head brakeman, who'd spent most of his trip from Fort Smith popping in and out of the caboose.

"Just wanted to say thanks for the ride," Longarm told the brakeman when he came within speaking distance. "If I'd've had to wait for a passenger train, I'd've lost a full day."

"Glad to oblige a lawman, Marshal," the brakeman replied. "That's about the only way us railroaders say thanks to you fellows for saving our bacon when there's a train holdup."

"Now, if you'll just tell me how I can get into town

from here, I'll be on my way," Longarm went on.

"Well, the best way is to just walk on alongside the tracks to about the middle of the yard here. There's a sorta road that'll take you to town," the head brakeman answered. "It's not quite a mile. If you want to ride, you'll have to keep on walking down the rails till you get to the passenger depot. There's always a hack or two there, but the depot's so close to the middle of town that all you'd be getting is a lift to the hotel. The hackmen don't come out here to the freight yards looking for fares."

"I don't guess I'll have any trouble," Longarm went on. "I have to find the Ranger that's on duty here, too. My chief in Denver wired me to pick up a prisoner they're holding."

"You'll find him at the police station if he's in town," the trainman said. "He's got a little office there. But he's out on some kind of Ranger business most of the time."

"Well, wherever he is, I'll likely manage to scrape him up sooner or later," Longarm told the brakie. "Thanks again for the ride."

Swinging his rifle with each long stride he took, Longarm walked beside the tracks until he reached the graveled road that the trainman had described. Looking along it in both directions he could see the yellow glow of lamplight coming form the windows of several distant houses, and decided quickly that the lights must mark the direction he'd need to take to reach the town. He shifted his rifle, resettled his saddlebags over his shoulder, and started toward the lights.

Judging by the dark houses he passed after reaching the outskirts of town, Longarm decided that most of Waco's residents were still sleeping. He strode past the unlighted dwellings until he saw light streaming from the top and bottom of a set of swinging doors, pushed through the batwings and looked around him. An aproned barkeep was leaning on an elbow behind the bar, and a drunk sleeping off his liquor was sprawled in a chair at one of the tables.

Except for this badly matched pair, the saloon was deserted. Longarm's boot heels thumping on the floor as he crossed to the bar aroused the barkeep, but did not disturb the drunk. At the bar, Longarm tossed a half-dollar on the mahogany.

"Maryland rye," he said. "And if I got a choice beyond that, I'd enjoy a tot of Tom Moore."

"You're in bourbon country now, mister," the barkeep told him. "I got just one bottle of rye whiskey in the place here, but it ain't Moore. And I ain't poured a drink out of it for something like three months."

"Then it's about time for you to pour another one," Longarm said. He took out one of his long slim cigars and lighted it as the barkeep turned and began looking along the back of the bar. He reached the far end before grunting with satisfaction and reaching for a bottle. When the man returned carrying the almost-full bottle, Longarm glanced at the label.

"Well, that's Pennsylvania liquor, but I guess it'll have to do me," he said. "Go on and pour." After he'd taken a sip of the whiskey and found it was not as bad as he'd expected, he went on, "What time does this town start stirring?"

"Why, that sorta depends, friend. Right now the farmers are waiting for the cotton to pop the bolls before they start picking, and all the schools are closed down for the summer, and none of the churches are having a revival, so there's not much to get anybody going early.

45

It's likely to be a little while after sunup before you see folks beginning to move."

Longarm tossed off the whiskey while the barkeep was rambling on. He refilled his glass before the man had finished his reply and asked when he fell silent, "I guess your police station shuts up at sundown and don't open till sunup, then?"

"I'd say that depends, too, mister. But if you was to be close by the station around daybreak, you'd likely find that Frank—Frank Glenn, that is, our chief of police—was starting to work about then."

"Is he the police force and the chief, too?"

"Oh, not by a long shot! He's got two men working for him. Frank's the one that generally opens the station up of a morning, though."

"How about a hotel? Is there more than one here?"

"Why, doggone it, there's three! Waco's not no hick town, mister! Not since the railroad come through about five or six years ago, it ain't! Now, we got just about every kind of store here that you can put a name to, and folks can buy about anything they need without having to go get it in Fort Worth or San Antone! And that ain't the half of it! Why, we got the female seminary and the new men's normal school and the black folks has even got them a seminary of their own! I tell you, friend, this town's likely to get as big as Fort Worth is in a few more years!"

"Now, that's real interesting," Longarm said, nodding. "Suppose you were a stranger here in Waco, like I am. Which one of them three hotels would you be likely to stop at?"

"I'd say the Sampson House, first off. It's right down in the middle of town. Big two-story place on the corner of Franklin and Fourth. No way you can miss it, even if you're a stranger here. Got a cafe right next door to it, if you're in a mind for breakfast."

"Which I am," Longarm said. "My belly button's rubbing on my backbone, so I better be moseying along."

He put his glass down on the bar. The saloonman picked up the half-dollar Longarm had put on the mahogany when he ordered his drink, opened the till drawer and dropped it in, took out a twenty-five-cent piece and a nickle, and shoved them across to Longarm.

"Stop in again when you're in the neighborhood," he said. "I got an idea from that Winchester you're toting and the six-gun on your hip and from the questions you been popping at me that you're some kind of lawman."

"Deputy United States marshal," Longarm told him. "Outa the Denver office. I've been on a case up in the Indian Nation and just stopped here in Waco because I got a wire from my chief telling me to swing by here on my way back to pick up a prisoner that your police chief's holding for us."

"That'd likely be the crook they call One-finger Carter," the barkeep replied. "Except the last I heard, they was still keeping him locked up in the jail over at Salem."

"Salem?" Longarm said frowning. "Where's that?"

"Oh, it's a little wide spot in the road about six or seven miles from here. Percy Moore—he's the constable there—arrested this fellow you're after not too long back. They caught him trying to bust into the church. Ol' Perc said he figured this Carter fellow needed a few dollars real quick and thought he might find some collection-plate money, seeing it was on a Sunday night that they caught him."

"And did he steal some church money?"

"Naw. Perc was passing by and caught him while he was just crawling into the church through a window he'd busted open. They got a little jail there, but they don't have a court or judge in town, so Perc's holding onto this fellow till he finds out some more about him, where he might be wanted and all like that. I guess that's why you're heading there, to pick him up for something he done someplace else."

"What the Federal government wants this fellow Carter for is robbing a U.S. Mail coach on the Union Pacific somewhere close to Ogallala."

"He'd get more time for that than just for trying to break into a church in a little bitty town like Salem," the barkeep said with a nod. "Looks like old Perc was right."

"Damned if I don't think you know more about the case I'm here on than I do myself," Longarm said. "How'd you come to know so much about it?"

"Why, Salem's a real strong church-town," the barkeep explained. "The folks there won't let a saloon open up in town, and some of the menfolk that live there drop in here for a quick swallow when they're in Waco. They don't dare go to one of the big saloons downtown, because they're afraid somebody that knows 'em might see 'em push through the batwings."

"So they come out here where they can bend their elbow on the sly, is that it?"

"That's about the size of it. And I guess that you being a lawman yourself, you know that after a man's had a few he ain't always real careful about what he says."

"And that's how you got in on all this?"

"Sure. Why, hell, mister, if I blabbed about half of what I hear the customers talking about on your side of

48

this bar, there'd be a lot of men in Waco—and Salem, and some other little places like it, I guess—that'd get walloped by their women folk with a frying pan every time they step in their houses."

Longarm smiled. "I'm not going to argue about that." He picked up his rifle and saddlebags. "Well, thanks for the information. I'll mosey on into town and have a bite to eat, then see if I can find your police chief."

When Longarm passed the little building that bore the sign POLICE STATION over the door, there was no sign of life inside. He tried the door, found it was locked, and walked on to the Sampson House. After signing the guest register and depositing his saddlebags and rifle in the second-floor room to which he was assigned, he sought the restaurant next door.

Bacon and eggs and two cups of strong black coffee later, he strolled back to the police station. This time the door was standing ajar. He pushed through it and entered. Across a small barren lobby there were two doors, one bore the sign CHIEF. Longarm stepped up to it and knocked.

"It's not locked," a man called from inside, "Come on in."

Behind a desk piled high with rumpled papers, a grizzled man sat holding a thick file-folder. He was shirtsleeved, his coat draped over the back of his chair, and sat a little sideways to accommodate the holstered revolver that was belted around his waist. A pipe was clamped between his teeth and around its stem he asked, "Looking for somebody, mister?"

"If you're Frank Glenn, I've found who I came to see."

"I'm Glenn. What's on your mind?"

"My name's Long, Chief. Custis Long. Deputy U.S. marshal outa the Denver office."

"Oh, sure," Glenn said nodding. "The one they call Longarm. I've heard about you, but somehow we never got acquainted before now." He laid the file on his desk and extended his hand. After the handshake, he waved to a chair that stood against the wall. "Pull it up and get comfortable while you tell me what's brought you here to Waco."

"It's not going to take but a minute to tell you why I'm in the neighborhood," Longarm said as he settled into the chair. "I have to pick up a prisoner that's in jail at Salem and take him back to Denver with me. I figured I'd better just stop by and say hello before I go pick him up, and find out the easiest way to get to Salem while I'm here."

"Glad you did. This prisoner you're talking about, I'd guess he's the fellow that tried to rob the church in Salem? One-finger Carter?" Glenn asked. When Longarm nodded, he went on, "I suppose I'm the one to blame for you being sent here."

"Now, that's interesting," Longarm said. "How'd you get mixed up in it?"

"Why, when I found out about Carter being arrested, his description sorta rang a bell, and I sent a wire to Ranger Headquarters in Austin. Didn't bother to check things out with old Percy in Salem before I did that, and he was just a mite riled because I butted into his case."

"From everything I gathered, they don't have much of a case against Carter in Salem," Longarm said.

Frank Glenn's frown matched Longarm's as he nodded and said, "That bothered me, too. He didn't manage to steal anything that I've heard about, but the people over there act like he'd robbed a bank—except that they don't have a bank in Salem to rob."

"From what little I've heard about the place, they don't have a lot of anything else in Salem, either," Longarm observed.

"Salem's not much of a town," Glenn agreed. "It's too close to Waco for anybody with any sense to put in a store or a bank or other business. And the people there are funny, too. Standoffish, most of them. This religion they've got isn't like any I've run into before."

"Well, be that as it may, I've got to go get my prisoner and haul him to Denver," Longarm said.

"They'll be looking for you, I suppose?"

"They're bound to know I'd be coming after him, or Billy Vail wouldn't've sent me all this way."

"You don't have much farther to go, though. Salem's about seven or eight miles northeast of here, and there's only one road in that direction. It's not much of a road, because it's just what's left of an old trail that goes back to the days when the Texas Rangers were first organized to fight the Indians. The road went to the Ranger Station that used to be at Fort Parker."

"It won't be the first bad piece of road I been over," Longarm replied. "Oh, yes. There's one more thing I need to ask you about. Have you got a spare cell I can put this One-finger Carter into for the night?"

"Sure. We've got six cells in the jail, and unless it's something like the Fourth of July or Texas Independence Day—we call it San Jacinto Day around here—when we get more than our share of drunk and disorderlies, there's plenty of room."

"That'll be fine, then. I'll leave you an expense voucher to pay for his keep, so you won't be outa pocket. But I figure it I go on over to Salem this morning, I can bring the prisoner back today, and then me and him will go out tomorrow on the first train north that connects up with one for Denver."

Glenn nodded.

Longarm stood up, saying, "I'll be moving on, then. Maybe if I get started right off, I can be back before it gets too late. I guess there's a livery stable here in town where I can hire a nag for me and one for him to ride?"

"Oh, sure. That won't put us out a bit, Long. And as for the horses, do you happen to know where the Sampson House is?"

"If I don't, I better find out real fast, because that's where I'm staying."

"Well, there's a livery stable on the street that runs in back of the hotel, and right behind the hotel building there's a livery stable. A fellow named Pete Gretch runs it, and he can be downright cantankerous sometimes. But you tell Pete I sent you over to him, and I'm sure he'll fix you up."

"Good. I'll mosey on over there, then, and be on my way. You might tell you men to be looking for me, in case you're not around when I get back later on and bring you my prisoner to lock up overnight."

"I'll do that," Glenn said. "They'll have a cell waiting."

Longarm strolled through the morning-quiet town back to the hotel and the livery stable behind it. Apparently he'd caught the liveryman on one of his better days, for he got the two horses that he requested and within a half hour after leaving the police station was on his way to Salem.

He followed the road that Frank Glenn had warned him would be more trail than road. Its dirt surface shunned the high grades. It wound around the uphill

52

stretches rather than surmounting them, though the up-grades were easy, and the ruts cut in earlier years by the wheels of the loaded wagons bringing new settlers to the region were shallow. The day was bright, the breeze cool, the branches of the pin-oak trees and the lower growth of sprawling mesquite thickets barely rippling as the wind rose briefly and faded.

Longarm saw Salem almost an hour before he reached it. The little town that was his destination lay away from the road a mile or so, and from the higher slope the road followed Longarm could see the winding, narrow wagon-road that led to it. The town stood near the center of a shallow, broad green trough that at one time had probably been the bed of some wide, massive and long-forgotten river.

Neatly laid out squares and rectangles between small clusters of a house, barn, sheds, or stable filled the valley. There were no fences that Longarm could see, but narrow wagon-trails between the fields marked the boundaries of the farms that stood cheek-by-jowl in the wide valley, a farmhouse near the center of each patchwork in the fields of growing crops.

Near the center of the patchwork he could see his destination. As Frank Glenn had told him, Salem was not much of a town. The steeple of the church marked its center. The narrow strip of road that led to it from the main road which Longarm was now following ended somewhere close to the church. Through the sparse foliage of scattered live-oak trees he could see a dozen or so houses, spaced far apart, making a loose cluster around the spire.

Soon after Salem came in sight, Longarm reached the fork in the road. One branch led to the town, the other stretched ahead across the rolling country until it vanished at the horizon. He reined his horse into the branch road and let the animal set its own pace as he fished a cheroot out of his pocket and lit it. Trailing a thin thread of smoke, he took stock of the neat farm fields that he rode past until he reached the small cluster of houses that constituted Salem.

Reining the livery horse to a slower pace, Longarm rode through the town. Its streets were totally deserted. He saw no one as he rode the length of the main street, then covered the two cross streets. The latter were only two blocks of modest, neatly painted dwellings surrounded by wide green lawns. Except for a small building that bore a sign GENERAL STORE, and the imposingly large clapboard church with its tall steeple, these made up the town.

He looked in vain for a sign of a city hall or town meetinghouse, then looked for a building that might be the jail, but none of the few structures that stood on the main street or the two cross streets bore a sign or any outward indication that they were anything other than family dwellings.

Puzzled by the deserted streets and the general air of sleepiness that hung over Salem, Longarm returned to the store. Its windows were shuttered, its door locked. He rapped at the door, and after he'd waited for several minutes it was opened a crack. A man peered out of the slit, then pulled the door open a bit wider, but still did not open it.

"If you're looking to buy something, you'll have to come back later," he said, his voice a half whisper. "I wouldn't've opened the door for you if I hadn't looked out and seen you're a stranger here."

"You mean you're closed up in the middle of the day

like this?" Longarm asked, his puzzlement showing in his voice.

"This is Meditation Time," the man inside replied. "Everybody in town is supposed to stop whatever they're doing and spend the noon hour meditating."

"Well, I'm a deputy U.S. marshal outa the Denver office, and I've come to pick up a prisoner," Longarm explained. "If you'll just tell me where the jail is, I'll go there and get him and be on my way."

"You'll have to wait until Meditation Time's over," the man inside said. "But seeing as you don't belong here, I guess it's all right for you not to be meditating. Go right on down the street past the church to the edge of town. You'll see a house with green trim and nothing much beyond it. That's Percy Moore's place. The jail's in behind his house. But I better tell you, Percy can't do anything till Meditation Time's over."

"How in blazes do you figure I'm going to know when that is?" Longarm asked.

"Oh, you can tell easy. Percy rings the church bell twice, so everybody in town will know."

"All right." Longarm nodded. "I'm obliged. I'll ride on down there and wait till I hear the church bell."

Without replying, the storekeeper closed the door and Longarm heard the metallic clicking of the lock. He stood there for a moment, gazing at the blank door, then walked down the low steps and remounted his horse. Reining it back to the street, he retraced his path past the church until he saw the green trim on the isolated white house as described by the storekeeper.

Forewarned, he made no effort to knock at the door, but sat in the saddle for a few minutes, then dismounted. He strolled back and forth in front of the house for what seemed a long time until he heard the church bell chime twice. He had only a short time longer to wait until he saw a man walking toward the house, and advanced to meet him.

"I reckon you'd be the town constable?" Longarm asked.

"Sure am, stranger. Percival Moore, at your service. What brings you to Salem?"

"My name's Long, Custis Long, deputy United States marshal outa the Denver office. I've come to take custody of that prisoner you got in jail here and take him back with me to Denver."

For a moment the town constable stood in silence, his mouth open, surprise written large on his features. Then he said slowly, "I'm real sorry, Marshal Long, but there's bound to be some kind of mix-up. I haven't got any prisoners at all in the lockup, let alone one that's supposed to go anyplace with you or anybody else."

# Chapter 5

For a moment, Longarm stared at the constable, then said slowly, "Now, maybe there's some kind of a mix-up, but I don't see how there could be. My chief in Denver wired me to come get this fellow. One-finger Carter is his name. That was just a few days ago, right after I'd closed another case up in the Indian Nation. You mean you never got word from Denver to hold this fellow for me?"

"Oh, sure. We got a message from somebody named Vail up in Denver that this prisoner we had was wanted by the federals, but the trouble is, it got here a day or so too late."

"I guess you better tell me just what you mean by that," Longarm told Moore. "Are you saying you'd already let this Carter go free?"

"He's about as free as us human beings can get, Marshal. You see, Carter had already gone on to meet his maker by the time we got that telegram from Denver."

"That's what folks say when they talk about somebody who's died," Longarm said, his voice flat.

"If you want to put it thataway," Moore said nodding, "he's dead, all right."

"And buried, too, I guess?"

"Why, sure. That's about all you can do with a dead body, after the real spirit's gone home to the high heaven. Or to the other place, if he was a sinner like that Carter fellow seems to've been."

"What'd he do? Try to get away, and you had to shoot him to stop him?"

"Oh, no, Marshal Long. He wasn't kicking up no

57

fuss like that. I didn't lay nary a hand on him."

"Then I guess you better tell me what he died of."

"He just died," the constable replied.

Longarm saw that the constable didn't propose to volunteer any further information. "Nobody just dies," he said. "Not unless somebody kills 'em or they're too sick for a doctor to cure or they're real old and feeble and their time's come."

"Well, I guess Carter's time had come, then." Moore spoke slowly, borrowing Longarm's words. "When I looked in on him in the jail before I left to go to the house and go to bed myself, he was chipper as he'd ever been. The next morning when I unlocked the door to give him his breakfast he was stretched out stiff and stark, deader than a doornail."

"I don't suppose you asked around town to see if there'd been anybody seen prowling close to the jail?"

Moore shook his head. "I didn't have to go bothering anybody with a lot of questions, Marshal. The jail's in a storm cellar right over yonder in back of my house. I sleep light, and I'd know about it if there was anybody nosying around."

"You know, it ain't a bit of my business, but why in tarnation is the town jail in a storm cellar back of your house, when it's so far away from the rest of the town?"

"Well, sir, that goes back a ways," Moore replied. "When we was first settling up here in Salem and parceling out the land, I got my section of land late in the drawing."

"You drew straws to see who got what land?"

"Sure. It was the only way to do it fair and square. That's why I'm so far out of town here. But be that as it may, I'd dug me a big storm cellar over there back of

58

my house, and fixed it up fancy with a brick lining and a big heavy door."

While he listened to Moore, Longarm slid a cheroot from his vest pocket, flicked a match into flame, and puffed the long thin cigar alight. Through a cloud of smoke he asked, "You turned your storm cellar into a jail?"

"Sure. It wasn't fit for much else. I wasn't about to waste all the sweat I dropped while I dug it, and it turned out that what we'd heard about the weather in this part of Texas wasn't true. There never has been a storm bad enough for me to use that cellar even a single time, so when the folks picked me out to be constable, I said I'd use my cellar for a jail and save the town the expense of building one."

"When you put it that way, it makes sense," Longarm admitted. "And it was in that cellar where you found Carter's dead body, is that right?"

"Right as rain."

"How long ago was it that he died?"

"Why, let's see, I guess it's going on a week, by now. Give or take a day either way."

"And you'd had him in jail for a week or so before he died, I understand."

"Something like that. I don't remember exactly how long it was, but we can go inside and look at my log-book if it's all that important."

"I can't figure out why he didn't tell you he was sick, or even felt bad?" Longarm frowned. "Because it don't seem natural to me that a man who hasn't got something pretty bad wrong with him would turn up his toes and pass on like that."

"Oh, it was real sudden, all right. Like I just told you, all I did was walk down the steps that morning,

59

and right away I seen that he'd cashed in his chips during the night."

"You're sure he looked all right the night before?" Longarm persisted. "And he didn't say anything about feeling bad?"

"Nary a word."

"Maybe one of the other prisoners killed him. They might've had a fight," Longarm suggested.

"There wasn't anybody but him in down there. Shucks, Marshal, there never has been a time when we've had more'n two or three men in our jail here. All we need is one cell."

"And one key? Which you'd've had all along?"

"Now, pull up there, Marshal Long! Don't go pointing no finger at me, just because I got a key to that cellar! The mayor's got his own key, so has Doc Parent, in case he's got to get in to treat a prisoner when nobody else is handy."

"I wasn't pointing at you, Moore," Longarm said quickly. "I'm just thinking out loud to try to get things straight for myself. Now, I don't guess you called a doctor to find out how come this fellow Carter died so sudden?"

"I ain't a plumb fool, Marshal. I done my best, but the only doctor closer than Waco is Doc Parent. When I tried to get hold of him a little while after I found the crook's body, he was way out at the Simmes place where Miz Simmes was birthing. Anyways, it didn't take no doctor to see that Carter was dead, and you know yourself there's nothing under God's blue sky that a doctor can do for a dead man. All he could've done was tell us it was time to bury him. And that's just what he done when he got back to town."

"I got to admit you did the best you could," Longarm said after considering the constable's statement for a moment. "So it looks like my job's over before I ever got it started."

"I'm sorry you been put to a lot of trouble." Moore's voice didn't hold the sympathetic tone that his words called for. He went on, "But if you was to ask me, I'd say that all you can do is turn around and start back to Denver."

"That's about right. I've got to do one little chore first, though. I'll need a copy of Carter's death certificate to take back with me."

"Death certificate?"

"That's to prove Carter's dead."

"I've already told you he is. Ain't that enough?"

"It's enough for me," Longarm answered. "And Billy Vail—he's my chief in Denver—would take my word that a prisoner I was supposed to bring in just up and died even before I got my hands on him. The trouble is that Billy's got a boss back in Washington, and he's going to want more than that."

"This death certificate, it's for your boss's boss, then?"

Longarm nodded, then seeing that the constable still didn't quite understand, he went on, "Billy's got to send him a death certificate signed by the doctor that said Carter was dead. But I don't reckon that'll be too hard to get, will it? You did say it was a doctor that told you."

"Sure. Doc Parent. He's the only doctor we got here in Salem."

"All I need to do is find him, then. You can show me where his office is, and I'll stop by on my way outa town and tell him what I got to have. It'll only take a minute for him to fix me up one."

"I guess I can do that, all right," Moore said a bit hesitantly. "You go past the church about three houses,

61

and Doc Parent's house is the big gray two-story one with white trim. It'll be on the right-hand side as you go toward the Waco road."

"Thanks," Longarm said. "I'll leave you to your business now and get on with what I have to do."

"I don't guess you'll be coming back to Salem, after you get your paper from the doc?"

"Not likely. I'll have to get back to my office in Denver, even if I haven't got a prisoner to bring in."

"Sure. Well, I'm sorry you had to ride all this way out here for nothing, Marshal Long. But it's nobody's fault. I sure didn't look for that Carter fellow to up and die the way he did. I hope you ain't blaming me for it."

"Now, why'd I do that?" Longarm asked.

"Well, I, uh . . ." Moore's words trailed off into silence. Longarm said nothing, and the constable made a fresh start. He said, "It was just a fool notion that popped into my mind, I guess. Don't pay no attention to it. Just go ahead and find Doc Parent and have him write you out whatever it is you need to take back to your boss in Denver."

"I guess I better do just that," Longarm said with a nod. "Not much use in me wasting my time on a dead man. And thanks for your help, Moore."

"Don't mention it. I'm just glad I could set you straight."

Reining his horse around, the extra horse following, Longarm started back toward town. He pulled up at the house described by the constable. Below its knocker, the door bore a brass nameplate, JAMES PARENT, M.D. Dismounting, Longarm tethered his horse to the hitching post that stood in front of the house, then took the two steps to the porch with one stretched stride and tapped the knocker twice.

After he'd waited for what seemed to be an unduly long time, he knocked again. A moment later the door was opened by a young woman. She wore a flowered gingham dress with an apron over it. She looked to be in her early twenties. Her dark hair was pulled back into a knot low off the back of her neck. She had high cheekbones and a short straight nose. Her lips were full and her chin was squared and firm. She looked at Longarm, a puzzled frown forming on her face.

"Why, you don't live here in Salem. I'm sorry I took so long, but I was—" She stopped and started again. "Are you looking for my father?"

"If he's the doctor, I am. My name's Long, ma'am. I'm a deputy United States marshal, outa the Denver office."

"And you've been hurt or taken sick?"

"Why, no. I got some business with Dr. Parent. Is he home?"

"I'm afraid not. But, well, I suppose you might as well come in. Maybe your business is something I can help you with."

"I don't reckon that's likely," Longarm replied. "But if the doctor's going to get back pretty soon, maybe you'd let me wait for him."

"I don't—" She stopped short, shrugged, and went on. "I guess so. Besides, if you're a stranger here you won't find anywhere else to wait." She stepped aside to let Longarm enter the hall and closed the door. Then she went on, "My name's Ellie, Marshal Long. Please go on in the parlor and sit down, it's through that door on your right-hand side." As she followed Longarm into the parlor she repeated, "I just don't have the least idea when father will be back, so I hope you're not in a hurry to see him."

"What I've got to ask him about won't spoil a bit if I

don't hear it for a while," Longarm assured her. He was removing his hat and looking around the parlor as he spoke. It was obvious that the doctor was doing quite well, even in a town as small as Salem. The room was furnished quite elegantly. A soft-toned Axminster carpet covered the floor, the wallpaper was a pattern in complementary stripes, and the furniture was of a set consisting of a horsehair-upholstered sofa and three chairs. Bright chromolithographs hung on the side walls, and lace curtains shimmered at the windows of the outside wall.

Longarm's inspection was completed in a very few seconds. As he turned to sit down in one of the chairs, he said to Ellie, "You and your folks sure have a nice place here."

"Why, thank you. But our family's just Father and me. My mother died when I was just a little baby."

"Well, now, that's too bad."

"It was a long time ago," she went on, "while we were moving here to Salem from the East. I don't really remember her, except what Father's told me about her. The ladies that were in the wagon train we were traveling with sort of brought me up."

Longarm recognized that Ellie's quickly given personal history stemmed from the loneliness shared by many women living in small isolated settlements. Many, perhaps most of them, met strangers so rarely that even immediately after their first chance encounter with someone they'd never seen before they talked readily and freely.

"So you and your daddy came here to Salem and settled down?"

"Oh, no, Marshal Long." Ellie shook her head. "There wasn't even such a place as Salem until Father and the others got here with the wagon train. I don't remember what it was like, of course, because I was still just a baby, but I've heard the older folks talking about what it was like."

"You and your daddy's friends started the town, then?"

"Yes. Texas had so much land that needed settling they were putting advertising in a lot of papers back East—about how they'd give a lot of land free to people who bought even a little bit of it. I've heard Father and his friends talk about how they were having a hard time making crops on the worn-out land they had back East, so they just up and moved."

"I'd guess a lot of the people who made that trip are still around to talk about it," Longarm nodded.

"Quite a few. There's the Lanes and the Carters and the Moores—except poor old Percy's wife passed on about two years ago—and the Masons and—" Ellie stopped short, shook her head, then went on. "I don't know why I'm rattling on this way, telling you about people you've never heard of before and can't really be interested in. I'm sorry, Marshal Long."

"There's not any need for you to be, Miss Parent. They're all friends of yours, almost family, like you said. I reckon after everything them folks and your daddy went through together, you sorta feel like you're all kinfolk."

"Yes, I suppose we do." Ellie looked past Longarm to glance out the window and went on, "I keep looking for Father to get back. He should be here by now. But as long as you're waiting, would you like a cup of coffee?"

"Why, that'd be right nice, Miss Ellie, if it's not going to put you to a lot of trouble."

"None at all. I keep a pot hot on the kitchen stove all the time, because Father enjoys it so much."

"Then I'd be happy to sip at a cup."

Ellie vanished into the other part of the house and returned in a few minutes carrying a small tray that held two cups of coffee. She gave one to Longarm, took one herself, placed the tray on the long narrow table that stood along one wall, and settled down into a chair facing him.

"I thought it'd be nice to have a cup myself, so if you don't mind, I'll join you while we wait for Father," she told him. "It's kind of a treat for me to talk to a visitor who's not hurting or all cut up or shot up."

"I wouldn't think there'd be many that had got shot in a nice quiet little town like this one," Longarm told her. "But from what I've seen, every place has got a few troublemakers."

"Yes. Of course, the town's got a law against it, but men do fight now and then, even here in Salem." While Ellie was speaking, hoofbeats sounded outside and a horse nickered. She said, "That's Father coming home now. His horse always does that when he starts for the stable."

"Then I'll get my business with your daddy fixed up and be on my way," Longarm said.

He stood up just as footsteps thunked in the hall, and a man's voice called, "Ellie? Where are you, my dear?"

"In the parlor, Father. There's a gentleman here to see you."

Dr. Parent came in. He was shedding his long linen duster as he entered. He said to Ellie, "I'll take care of the new patient, my dear. You'll be wanting to get on with your housework, I'm sure."

"Yes, Father," she replied. "But Marshal Long—"

"Run along, now," the doctor told her. "It's not proper for a young lady to be in the room while I'm talking with a patient, especially a male patient."

66

Ellie looked from her father to Longarm. She began again, "Father, this gentleman—"

"This gentleman will explain to me himself what's wrong with him," Parent said. "Now, do as I say, Ellie." He watched as his daughter left the room, then turned to Longarm.

"I'm sorry to keep a sick man waiting, sir, but I'm sure that Ellen explained why I wasn't here."

"She sure did," Longarm said. "Except that she was trying to tell you I'm not sick."

"You're not?"

"If I am, I don't know it," Longarm replied.

"Then why did you come looking for me?"

"My name's Long, Doctor, and I'm a deputy federal marshal outa the Denver office. I came here to Salem to pick up that prisoner your constable had in jail, because he robbed a U.S. Mail coach a while back. So when my chief up in Denver heard he'd been arrested here—"

"Marshal Long," the doctor broke in, "the only prisoner we've had in the Salem jail recently died while he was there. Is he the man you're talking about?"

Longarm nodded. "One-finger Carter's what folks call him. And I already know he died sudden a few nights ago."

"That's right," Parent agreed. "We buried the poor devil the same day that our jailer found he'd passed away."

"So I've been told," Longarm replied. "Which means I can't take him back to Denver, so I got to have a death certificate to take back instead."

"And that's why you've come to me, of course," the doctor said nodding. "Well, there won't be any problem. If you'll excuse me, I'll just step into my office and write out the certificate for you. It'll only take a minute."

"Go right ahead," Longarm said. "I don't mind waiting a bit."

True to his promise, Dr. Parent returned in a very short time, carrying a long white envelope. He handed the envelope to Longarm, saying, "Here you are, Marshal Long. As you see, I put the certificate in an envelope so it won't get soiled or crumpled while you're carrying it."

"That was right thoughtful," Longarm said. "Many thanks for your trouble, and tell Miss Ellie I said thanks to her, too, for the coffee she gave me. I'll be riding back to Waco, now."

Engrossed in the business that had brought him to Salem, Longarm had paid little attention to the passing of time. He stepped out of the doctor's house into the fast-waning day. The sun still hung above the horizon, but only a thin strip of blue sky lay between the two. The town's single street was as deserted as it had been during the noon hour. The sun's rays were still bathing the tip of the church steeple, but the long shadows of approaching dusk were spilling across the little community's single street as he tucked the envelope into the pouch on the inner flap of one of his saddlebags.

"Old son," he told himself, "you're going to have to mosey along at a pretty good clip if you aim to get back to Waco before it's too dark to see the road, and having that sunset in your face most of the way ain't going to help you none, either."

After he'd left the town and was riding along the road to its junction with the better-defined road leading to Waco, the sunset light was still bright enough for Longarm to see his way clearly. He reached the junction and reined the livery horse to the better-marked road that followed the bank of the long-dry riverbed, and on higher ground with the trees spaced farther apart, the light improved.

He'd covered the first mile or so after turning onto the main road when he first noticed the three riders streaking across the low ground from the direction of Salem.

*Now, that's a funny thing,* Longarm thought. *Why would they be cutting across open country that way and risk having a horse step in a pothole and maybe bust its leg when there's this pretty fair road for 'em to take? They must be in some kind of hurry to risk going across that gully so close to dark.*

Then his lawman's fine-honed instinct began prodding. Veteran of many attacks and ambushes, Longarm knew that anything out of the normal could mean oncoming danger. The vagrant thought that had occurred to him a few seconds earlier took him another step forward.

*Things like that don't happen for no reason at all,* his fresh thought ran. *They got a reason for angling up toward this stretch of road, old son, and seeing as you're the only one on it, that reason's got to be you.*

Longarm did not pause to question his instinct. He dug his heels into the flanks of the livery horse, but the extra horse had no rider to spur it to a better pace. Longarm's mount did its best, but hampered by the drag of the riderless animal it could not move a great deal faster. The three riders were spurring their mounts now, and he could see that they were going to be within rifle range very soon.

As though the trio had been intercepting Longarm's thoughts, they were sliding rifles out of their saddle scabbards. Longarm freed his own Winchester and levered a cartridge into its chamber. Before he could raise the rifle to fire, red muzzle-blasts, spurted from the weapons of two of the mysterious riders. The range was still extreme, and their bullets kicked up dust fifty yards short of him, but now he knew positively what his instinct had been silently saying to him since he'd gotten his first view of them.

Knowing that he still had several minutes before the man approaching him could shorten the range between them, Longarm did not reply to their shots. He gave his full attention to sweeping the landscape with his eyes, straining to pierce the onrushing dusk, looking for a spot that might give him some cover, and even the odds between himself and the pursuing riders.

Ahead, the road curved around a low hillock that was silhouetted against the western horizon. Seeing at a glance that within a few moments the rising ground would be between him and his attackers, Longarm yanked the lead rope of his extra horse free and dug his heels into the sides of his mount.

Now that it'd been relieved of the spare horse's drag, the animal sped up. Though it would provide poor cover at best, the rise ahead was the only spot he saw that might help him elude his attackers. Bending low in the saddle, pounding his heels on the livery horse's sides, he rode hard for the hump.

# Chapter 6

As he reached the low hillock, Longarm saw that its top was covered by a thick stand of low-growing huisache. He judged the shrubs to be just a bit less than shoulder-high, scant cover at best, but better than no cover at all. He spurred up to the top of the rise and rolled out of his saddle as he reined in. The shrubs were not quite as high as he'd thought them to be, but they stood tall enough to hide him and his mount from a man looking up from below.

Looping his horse's bridle around the closest huisache branch, Longarm edged forward to take fresh stock of his situation. On the gently undulating prairie below the rise, the three attackers were clearly visible now. Two of them were spurring ahead, reining apart as they rode, the gap between them widening as they approached the base of the hump. Having faced much the same situation before in country that was similar, Longarm read their intention at a glance.

At the base of the hillock the pair would split up, and the third man might make one of two moves: He could wait until his companions where in place to ride uphill and follow them, or simply stay where he was and wait for them to flush their quarry out. Then, Longarm would be in the center of a constantly closing triangle, facing three-to-one odds. He'd faced greater odds before, and had no qualms about facing them now, nor did he worry about adding another gun battle to his long string of such encounters. The thought shaping his decision now and overriding all other considerations was that he needed to stay alive and finish his job.

Glancing across the rolling prairie, he saw that the third man had already slowed his pace, while the other two were spreading out in opposite directions, galloping around the base of the mound. There was no need for Longarm to calculate the odds against him. He'd done all the arithmetic long ago while facing other adversaries.

He knew that his best chance was to ride down the low mound and take on the rider there, who was now reining in at its base to give his companions time to get into the position that would allow them to come upon Longarm from the rear. In a moment Longarm heard one of the men who'd ridden around the base of the hillock call to his companions.

"He's holed up on top someplace! He sure didn't keep on down the Waco road," the man yelled.

"He didn't double back, neither," the other shouted. "Now all we got to do is spook him outa that huisache brush up on top of the hump! Once he breaks cover, one of us will get him!"

"We better move, then," the first man said. "He can't go no place but down. If we go up from this side and Coley takes care of his job on the other side, we're sure to nail the son of a bitch!"

"I'm right with you!" his companion called. "Let's move!"

Longarm heard a thudding and scraping of hoofbeats as the men started up the hillock. He tried to pinpoint the locations of the pair by the noises they were making—the thunking scrape of the horses' hooves, the rustling of the thick, close-growing huisache that was his screen as his pursuers pushed through it. They were too close together and too near him now, and he was unable to separate the two sets of noises as the pair rode up the slope.

72

Hoping to gain time and in the same stroke reduce the odds against him, Longarm returned to his horse. He could hear the brush crackling and rustling more loudly now as the men drew closer together on the conical hump of the rise. Untying his horse's reins, he led the animal on a zigzag course through the thick huisache growth, moving as quietly as he could, heading in the direction of the man whose voice had sounded loudest when they spoke last, and whose progress was now marked by the most clearly audible brush-crackles.

Suddenly the voice of one of his pursuers arose over the rustling that seemed to come from everywhere on the hillock. "Hey, Manny!" the distant man called. "You seen hide or hair of him yet?"

Longarm froze when the man addressed as Manny replied, for his voice seemed to be only inches away. "Not a sign!" he called in reply to his companion's question. "And I take it you ain't either."

Longarm was dividing his attention between listening to the exchanges between the two men searching for him and scanning the ground close by, looking for a thick, low-growing stand of bushes or a dense patch of the prairie grass that grew calf-high in the spaces the brush hadn't yet preempted. He knew he had very little time, and though the men searching for him had stopped moving while they talked, the one called Manny was dangerously near.

"Well, dammit, he's gotta be up here somewhere, even if we ain't heard him moving around or seen hide nor hair of him!" the more distant man answered. "And this prairie wool sure ain't tall enough to hide him. Seems like the ground just opened up and swallowed him!"

"He didn't head for the other side of this hump, either," Manny called back. His voice sounded even closer to Longarm than it had when he'd spoken before. "We'd've heard Pinkey cutting down on him if he had."

"We just got to keep on looking," the second searcher shouted. "There ain't all that many places where a man can hide up here on this rise!"

"We sure better find him, Scott!" Mannie said. "You heard what the boss told us. That bastard's already done too much pokin' into things back in town. They want us to take him alive and hand him over to the quiet guns. They'll finish him off tonight, and then his body won't turn up and get folks started asking questions."

Longarm registered the remarks in his brain but had no time to waste trying to puzzle out their meaning. He could tell by the loudness of their voices that the two men were dangerously close to flushing him out of his scanty cover.

*Old son,* he thought, *it's root hog or die. You might as well get on with it, whichever way the chips fall.*

Swinging into his saddle, then bending low, he dug his heels into the flanks of the livery horse. Rested after its brief pause, the animal leapt forward. Brush crackled as he broke cover, and Longarm heard fresh shouts rising from the men who were searching for him.

"There he goes!" the man called Mannie shouted. "Swing this way, Scott!"

A rifle barked and the slug whistled for a moment, then the whistle died as it was deflected, but still the lead cut through the huisache uncomfortably close to Longarm's head. He tried to bend lower, to hide his progress, but the growth was too scanty and too low growing.

Another shot cut the air, but Longarm had passed the crest of the little hump of ground and was starting downhill so the slug from the rifle whistled above him.

As he bent forward in his instinctive reaction he slid his Colt out of his holster. A moment later he could see in broken silhouette the figure of the third man looming as a blob here and there between breaks in the waving huisache branches.

Now Longarm knew that he had a least a tiny edge over his pursuers, a small but important advantage. The higher velocity bullets of the rifles they were using would be deflected by the underbrush unless luck opened a gap for a clear shot, but the heavier slug from his Colt with its lower muzzle velocity would crash on through the thin huisache and find a target.

Raising the pistol, Longarm triggered off two quick shots. Though the form of the man who was his target was obscured by the undergrowth, Longarm saw him jerk in the saddle and then sag forward as the Colt's lead ripped into him. Changing direction would endanger the small but vital margin Longarm was ahead of the men who were threshing through the huisache thicket behind him. He did not twitch his reins, but crashed through the brush within arm's length of the man who'd taken his lead just as he was crumpling sidewise in his saddle.

Rushing straight downhill now through the thinning huisache growth the livery horse was picking up speed. Behind him Longarm heard a shout.

"That bastard's shot hit Pinky! I got to stop and help him!" Mannie called.

"Help him, hell!" Scott called back, his voice rising louder than before above the diminished thrashing and cracking of the huisache. "If we don't catch up to that damn federal marshal and bring him back, nobody's going to help us!"

Mannie's hesitation delayed Longarm's pursuers only briefly, but it had been enough to give Longarm a tiny edge over the pair chasing him. Passing through the last of the undergrowth, Longarm saw the level prairie stretching in front of him. He kicked the livery horse ahead as a shout from above told him that his pursuers had broken through the brush and seen him.

Longarm drummed his heels against his horse's barrel and the animal responded, but not eagerly. It picked up its pace, but the wild dash through the brush seemed to have taken something out of the animal. The horse was not yet panting, but Longarm could feel an occasional heaving of its sides, and now and then its skin-muscles twitched. It would not be long, he knew, before he'd be forced to stop and rest the animal.

He looked back and saw one of his pursuers break free of the huisache and start down the short strip that still slanted down to the level prairie. The other man emerged almost at once. He called to his companion, who turned to look back, then reined his horse down to allow the second man to catch up. Longarm could tell that they were either arguing or planning, but he had no time to waste trying to decide which. He toed the livery horse ahead and started at a gallop for the horizon, into the reddening glare of the beginning sunset.

He'd covered only a half mile or less and was still out of range of his pursuers' rifles when his horse began to breathe with an occasional wheeze in its throat. Having covered enough miles straddling enough different horses to understand the significance of the animal's rough raspy inhalations, Longarm began to study the terrain ahead more carefully. He was now searching for a spot of his own choice where he could stand and fight instead of being forced to defend himself wherever the animal could no longer maintain its present pace.

No matter where he looked there was no cover on the

barren prairie—no trees, no broken ground, no hills nor gullies. The tall grass that rippled everywhere around him presented a surface that was as smooth as a huge lake or ocean. The sun was at the horizon now, and Longarm knew that if he could stand off the men chasing him for as little as a quarter of an hour, darkness would provide the cover he needed so badly to help him escape his pursuers.

Swiveling in his saddle he looked back at the men chasing him. They were not shooting now, though neither of them had put their rifles back in the saddle sheaths that were on each horse. His own mount had recovered from its spell of wheezing and gasping, but Longarm needed no one to warn him that the recovery was almost certainly a temporary one. He still held the same thin lead, but he was sure that when his horse slowed down even a little bit the thin-edged advantage he was now holding onto would quickly be lost.

Longarm quickly reached the conclusion that prolonging his running would solve nothing. Without slowing his pace he drew his Colt, ejected the spent cartridges in its cylinder, and thumbed fresh loads from his belt loops to replace them. This time he did not leave an empty chamber on which to rest the revolver's hammer.

Holstering the Colt, he slid his Winchester from its saddle scabbard and slipped fresh rounds into the loading port until the magazine was refilled. He did not restore the rifle to its saddle scabbard, but kept it in his hand. A shot from the rifle of one of his pursuers neither hastened his methodical moves nor caused him to look back. Only when both weapons were fully loaded did he glance over his shoulder to check on the progress of the men chasing him.

Both still carried their rifles ready to fire, and while

he was watching, one of them brought the weapon to his shoulder. Longarm seized the unexpected opportunity when one of his adversaries was occupied with aiming and his companion was turning to watch the shot triggered off.

Getting a firm grip on the reins of his mount with his free hand, Longarm jerked them sharply to one side. The horse's head twisted around, and it broke stride. Then it lurched forward with a surprised snort and its front hooves struck one another as it tried to obey the unexpected tugging. Tripping as its hooves tangled, the animal tottered for a split second, loosed a loud protesting neigh when it realized it was toppling, then plunged down to earth in a tangle of threshing hooves.

In the instant before yanking the reins, Longarm had slipped his feet from the stirrups. As the horse fell he held onto the saddle horn with his gun hand until the last minute, when it was possible for him to move without having a leg trapped under the falling horse. As his feet touched the ground he let his downward momentum bend his knees, then kicked himself free of the toppling animal.

For a moment the horse neighed with angry shrillness as it fell, its hooves flailing the air. Then its panic subsided and its neighs died away as it tried to roll over as the first move to getting back on its feet again. Longarm had anticipated this, too. He had his hand locked firmly around the animal's headstall and was forcing the horse to hold its head down and remain in its position, prone on one side.

Without releasing his grasp, Longarm took the single long step that put him between the horse's legs. He'd released his grip on the rifle after hitting the ground. Just as he bent to pick up the weapon a shot rang out from one of the riders pursuing him. The slug whistled past Longarm's head and sailed on to thunk into the earth behind him.

Longarm fired back, not taking time to shoulder his rifle, but handling it like a pistol and hip shooting without really aiming, using only one hand and triggering off his shot in a single lightninglike move.

Longarm proved to be a better shot than the man who'd fired at him. His lead went home, striking the rider in the shoulder and knocking him out of his saddle. He landed limp and with a thud.

His companion was close enough to join the shooting now. Longarm saw him swinging his revolver around and dropped flat an instant before the rider squeezed off his shot. The bullet whizzed overhead and raised a puff of dust from the ground beyond Longarm's equine fortress.

Sheltered for the moment, if only barely, Longarm took time to aim his next shot. Over the sight blade of his Colt he saw the still-mounted pursuer shouldering his rifle. Before the man could bring down the barrel of the long-gun for an aimed shot, Longarm closed his finger on the Colt's trigger. The heavy slug found its mark. The rider's second shot was triggered by his dying reflex and the bullet from his rifle sailed up into the fast-darkening sky. The rifle fell from his hands as he toppled backward and slid lifeless out of his saddle to fall in a heap on the ground.

"Don't shoot again, mister!" the man who'd taken Longarm's first dose of lead called. "I ain't about to give you no more trouble! Look!"

While Longarm watched hawklike, his Colt ready in his hand, the fallen man tossed his rifle as far as he could throw it. Then, moving slowly and carefully, he drew his revolver, using only his thumb and forefingers to slide the weapon out of its holster and send it sailing through the air to join his rifle.

"I ain't sure you're worth keeping alive," Longarm told him, his voice flat. "Let's get something clear before we say another word. You come from Salem, don't you?"

"You oughta know that. You seen us riding out after you."

"Maybe I just wanted to hear you say it," Longarm replied, his voice steely hard. "So if you come from there, you oughta know what's going on."

"I don't, mister. I'm just doing what I was told to. I learned a long time ago that if I didn't they'd set the quiet guns on me."

This was the second time Longarm had heard that phrase. He asked, "Just who might them quiet guns be?"

"You're asking the wrong man. All I know is that they're real, and if you get crossways of 'em, you're as good as dead."

"Now that don't make sense," Longarm said. "There ain't any such thing as a quiet gun unless it's one that's unloaded, and if you're the kind of man I got you ticketed for, you'll know that for a fact."

"Mister, since I been in Salem I've learned there's a lot of things I don't know much about, and that's just one of 'em. Anyways, I ain't going to be much good at telling you a damn thing unless I get a bandage around this bullet hole you put in me. I'm bleeding like a stuck pig."

For several moments Longarm did not reply, then he went on, "Well, now. You tell me if I'm wrong, but say I was to bandage you up and save you from bleeding to death, I'd want you to do something for me."

"All you got to do is name it. Only don't take too much time making up your mind what you want me to do. I'm getting weaker by the minute."

"I guess saving your life is worth you telling me everything you know about them quiet guns you talked about?"

"Everything I know's not a whole lot, but I'll sure tell you all I've seen and found out since I been in Salem."

"Reckon I'll settle for that," Longarm said. "Just as long as you don't lie to me, we got a deal. But that don't stretch to letting you off scot-free."

"Take me to jail if you've got to. Just don't let nobody get me back to Salem and them quiet guns."

"I'll guarantee you that much," Longarm promised. "Now, I'll pack that bullet hole to stop it from bleeding and tie a bandage around it. Then you and me are going to stay right here while I listen to what you have to say. We'll see what happens after you've finished talking."

"Anything that suits you. Only hurry up and get me wrapped up so I don't bleed to death."

Longarm worked swiftly and efficiently for the next few minutes. He cut off the wounded gunman's shirtsleeve at the shoulder seam and examined the twin holes that his rifle slug had made. They were both clean, the high-velocity rifle slug did not tear flesh as did the slower, softer bullet from the Colt.

Next he took a clean bandanna out of his saddlebags and shredded it into lint that he pressed into the gunman's wound to stop the bleeding. Then he split the shirtsleeve lengthwise and used half of it to make a bandage that would press the lint tight and immobilize the gunman's arm. The other half he knotted into a sling that would support the man's arm and keep it from moving and reopening the wound.

While Longarm worked, the wounded man gritted his teeth and bore the pain. He'd groaned and twitched a time or two when Longarm was packing the bullet hole with lint, but after he'd seen the flow of his blood stopped, he'd remained silent during the few minutes required to do the bandaging.

"All right," Longarm said as he pulled the last knot in the bandage tight and straightened up. He took out one of his slim cigars and lit it. "You're not going to die—not for a while, anyway. Now, start talking. And I guess the best way to begin is to tell me your name."

"Scott Coley," the prisoner replied. "And that's my real name. Folks who know me mostly call me Scotty."

"You know who I am, I guess?"

"Sure. You're the federal marshal they call Longarm. Of course, I'd heard about you before, but they was talking about you, back in Salem."

"When they sent you and them other two fellows out to kill me?" Longarm asked.

Coley nodded. "What they really wanted to do was have us bring you back to Salem. We told 'em we couldn't guarantee to do that, so they said do the next best thing if we had to and get rid of you."

"You and the two fellows that you were riding with, it sounds to me like you make a business outa killing people."

"We make a business—well, maybe I better say we made a business outa doing whatever we had to do that'd get us three meals a day and a few cartwheels to buy whiskey with."

Longarm's expression did not change when he heard Coley's confession. Gunmen, many of them survivors of the War Between the States, were commonplace throughout the still-unsettled West. He said, "You talked a couple of times about the quiet guns. Maybe you better tell me just what that means."

Coley was silent for a moment. Then he said, "I don't know how they do it, Marshal, but they shoot people in that place and nobody ever hears a gun go off."

Now it was Longarm's turn to be silent. His judgment told him that Coley was speaking the truth, as improbable as his statement seemed. He could tell from the outlaw's manner that he believed completely in the existence of the quiet guns, even if he was unable to explain them, and decided to change the line of his questioning and return to the quiet guns later.

Longarm asked his prisoner, "You're saying the folks in Salem make a business outa killing? Why, I got the idea from talking to 'em and looking around the town that they were a bunch of psalm singers."

"They are," Coley agreed. "But that don't stop 'em from stealing and killing and hiding out men that're on the dodge."

"Is that how you and your friends happened to tie up with 'em?" Longarm asked.

Nodding, the outlaw said, "Pretty much. Until we run up against you, we were getting along fine. Now, I guess that's the end of it."

"Not quite," Longarm replied. "But we'll talk about that later on. Get up and come along. We're riding into Waco."

# Chapter 7

From the lights that showed in windows of the houses they could see when they drew close to Waco, Longarm judged that most of the town's residents had retired for the night. Even across the expanse of crisscrossing rails that formed the railroad yards they could see that the streets were deserted. They'd had to keep their horses close-reined while crossing the maze of tracks, and when they'd glanced along the rails the yards had shown very little activity.

"I ain't bothered you with a lot of questions, Marshal Long," Coley said as they started across the barren stretch of land that stretched from the tracks to the first streets of the town. "I could tell you was busy thinking, and I was, too, most of the way here. But I'd sorta like to know what you're going to tell the Waco lawmen about me."

"Why, I imagine they'll know enough about you without me having to tell 'em anything," Longarm answered. "There's likely to be Wanted notices on you from quite a few places, if they don't want you for some job you pulled off here in town. They'll find a jail where there's a cell waiting for you, don't worry about that."

"Oh, that ain't what's been bothering me. I just don't want 'em to send me back to that storm-cellar-jail in Salem. It's the spookiest place I ever hid out in."

"So you said before. I guess the two we left dead out there on the prairie felt the same way?"

"They sure as hell did. Big Ed was getting ready to

pull out and Mannie wasn't none too happy."

"Wait a minute," Longarm said. "I didn't hear either one of them two called Big Ed. One of 'em was Mannie, the other one was Pinkie, if I recall."

"Now, Marshal, you know as good as I do that a man on the owl-hoot trail uses whatever name comes to mind when he's got a bunch of Wanteds out on him."

"Look here, Coley, if you and me are going to get anyplace, you got to start telling the truth," Longarm said sternly. "Now, I know there's a Wanted notice out on a fellow called Big Ed Blossom. Matter of fact, he's on our list up in Denver. Is he the one that was traveling as Pinkie?"

"That was him, all right," Coley admitted. "As for Mannie, that's Bill Menard. I'd've got around to telling you, when we have that talk you want."

"Well, soon as I can find a doctor to put a real bandage on that gunshot hole you got, you and me will sit down and you can tell me all about it," Longarm said. "And this time I don't want you to hold anything back on me."

They were approaching the YARD LIMITS sign. Even in the gloom the black lettering on the sign's white background could be made out clearly. Deeper in the yards, lights from the roundhouse and the freight-car maintenance sheds seeped up into the dark sky and contributed a bit to lessening the deep darkness. Its light enabled them to see that the street running along the yards was lined with shanties, most of them bearing the signs of having been abandoned after the railroad-construction boom ended.

At the far end of the street a gaslight glowed on a corner, and toward the center of the yards the all-night activity of the busy repair and maintenance crews was in full swing. From the roundhouse a quarter mile down the track an occasional clanging of hammers on metal sent a *rat-a-tat* out to disturb the quiet night, and still deeper into the yards the headlight of a switch engine poked a yellow cone into the midnight blackness.

Now and then the bobbing glow of a lantern carried by one of the switchmen caromed off the darkness like a firefly. The sounds of the shots that burst from the row of shanties across the wide road sounded like cap-pistol pops above the louder noises of the busy yards, but the bullets that kicked up the cindery gravel around the horses ridden by Longarm and Coley were very real indeed.

"Hit the dirt!" Longarm warned Coley as he rolled out of his saddle and drew his Colt in the same move. His actions were almost instinctive, born of long practice. His eyes were searching the blackness between the shanties for signs of movement, but he saw none.

"I'm..." Coley began, then the words ended in a gargling gasp as he pitched sideways off his horse and fell sprawling onto the cindery ground.

Another round of firing came from the shanties. This time Longarm could see gun flashes, three of them, widely spaced. He snapshot at the areas where the muzzle blasts had showed, but even as he triggered off his shots he knew that his chances of a hit with such blind shooting were very small indeed.

Only two shots replied to Longarm's fire. He was reloading his Colt when the reports split the night, and the red spurts from the ambushers' guns marked the spots where they were sheltered. Though he was sure he'd be wasting lead, Longarm sent a pair of slugs in the general direction of the areas where he'd noted the muzzle blasts.

He waited when he'd fired twice, his Colt ready, but no more shots came from the darkness across the wide street. Though he was reasonably sure that the mysterious assailants had gone, he stayed motionless. A yard or two from him, Longarm could hear Coley's labored breathing. When several minutes had dragged out and no more firing came from the shanties, he called to his prisoner, keeping his voice low.

"Coley? You all right?"

"Not so's you'd notice." Coley's voice was thin and strained and sounded muffled. "I taken a chunk of lead where it hurts."

"Lay still," Longarm said. "I'll crawl over and see what I can do."

Longarm crawfished across the sooty gravel to Coley's side. He could not see the outlaw plainly in the gloom, and since no more shots had come from the bushwhackers across the street, he decided it would be worth the risk to look. He took a match from his vest pocket and dragged his thumbnail across its head, closing his eyes before the match head burst into flame, then opening them slowly to prevent light blindness.

In the flickering light from the burning match Longarm saw a bloodstain spreading over the outlaw's shirtfront. The dark seepage of blood was also beginning to show high on Coley's arm, staining with a brighter, fresher crimson flow the bandage that he'd put on the man earlier.

"Think you can pull me through this one, too, Marshal?" the outlaw asked, straining to look down at the bandaged arm. His voice was edgy, but unwavering.

"Seeing as there's no time to waste trying to find a doctor at this hour of the night, it looks like I better have a try," Longarm replied. He was taking out his clasp knife as he spoke. He opened the largest blade and cut away the remaining sleeve of Coley's shirt, slit it lengthwise along the seam, then made a second lengthwise slit to give him two long strips of the closely woven fabric. As he knotted the strips together he warned the wounded outlaw, "You ain't going to be real comfortable when I pull on this, but there's no other way to do it, so clamp your jaws and hang on."

"Go ahead," Coley told him. "I can stand it."

Longarm slipped the improvised bandage between the outlaw's upper arm and chest, where the bullet hole was still welling blood with each breath Coley took. Planting his knees firmly, he pulled the strip of cloth tight. Coley gasped and winced with pain as the fabric pulled against his wound, but not a sound escaped his lips as the cloth cut into the flesh around its edges.

Holding the tension in the bandage, Longarm knotted it. A small bloodstain formed over the spot where the bullet had gone in, and Longarm strained his eyes through the gloom as he watched it spread. The stain stopped growing when it had covered an area that could easily be covered by a man's palm.

"It looks like I got the worst of the bleeding stopped," Longarm said. "If you just lay still and don't move, you might come out of it all right, but I can't make promises."

"Thanks," Coley gasped. Longarm could see that he was straining to breathe. "I know you didn't have to do anything to help me. I ain't going to forget it."

"Save the thanks till you see if I've done enough," Longarm told the wounded man. He took one of his long thin cigars from his pocket and lighted it before going on. "But if you were of a mind to help me, you might tell me a little bit about that bunch in Salem that you've been working for."

"A little bit like what?"

"Oh, how many of 'em there are. What they do. I know they got some kind of crookedness going on there, but I can't quite figure what, except that I've heard a couple of times about their quiet guns."

Coley started to say something, but only a gurgle came from his throat. He hawked and spat a gobbet of blood. Then he tried again and managed to say, "They got quiet guns, that's for sure, Marshal. Even if I didn't see anybody do it, I know for sure since me and Mannie and Big Ed first thrown in with 'em they've shot and killed three or four people, and nobody ever heard a gun go off."

"You mean they don't even try to cover up their killing?"

"They make sure nobody's looking on," Coley wheezed, "but they don't mind talking about what they do."

"You feel up to telling me what that is?"

"Don't take what I've guessed for gospel, Marshal. But the way me and Mannie and Big Ed figured, they rob the dead men."

"Rob the—" Longarm began, but broke off short when Coley gasped and choked and a spurt of blood shot from his mouth.

For a moment the outlaw worked his jaws as though he were trying to speak, but the gagging spurts of fresh blood choked off anything but its grisly gurgle. Longarm knew what was happening. He'd seen men die this way before when a bullet close to an armpit had pierced the large auxiliary artery and allowed the blood it carried to spurt into their lungs. He knew that Coley was quite literally drowning in his own blood, and knew also that there was no doctor alive who could be of any help to him.

"If you got a prayer to make, call it to your mind, Coley," he said. "There's not a thing me or anybody else can do for you."

Before Longarm had finished speaking, the outlaw's eyes had widened, and they seemed to open still wider when his body convulsed in a final shudder. Then he lay motionless as death stilled his quivering.

Longarm stood looking down at Coley's body for a moment before stepping back to where their horses stood. He led them up to the dead man. Lifting Coley's sagging, unwieldy body, he managed to get it across the saddle of the animal the dead outlaw had been riding. Mounting his own horse and leading Coley's he started through the deserted streets to the Waco police station.

As he'd expected it to be at that hour of the graveyard shift after midnight, the station was deserted except for the desk sergeant. Taking out his well-worn wallet before the sleepy sergeant could get fully awake, Longarm flipped it open to show his badge. "Maybe you've heard Frank Glenn say something about me," he said.

"Why, sure, Marshal Long. You're the one he calls Longarm."

"Folks do." Longarm nodded. "The reason I'm here is I got a body laying crossways of a horse outside."

"A dead body?"

"He sure as hell ain't going to move no more," Longarm told the policeman. "And to save you asking a bunch of questions, I didn't cut him down, but that's something else I'll talk about later on."

"I guess this body's got a name? Or did have?"

"Sure. Scott Coley. There'll be a Wanted flier someplace around the station here. But I figured on turning him over to you before I head for the Sampson House and catch up on my shut-eye."

"Sounds like you've been having trouble."

"A mite. This Coley fellow outside was one of three hired guns that started following me from Salem, and when me and him come outa the railroad yards there was a couple of bushwhackers waiting for us. That's when he took the bullet that finished him off."

"What about the men that jumped you? Was they friends of his, trying to get him away from you?"

"I doubt they were friendly to either me or him. They wouldn't've cut loose on us the way they did if they'd been trying to get him free. They were out to kill both of us, the way I got it figured."

"And they got away? How many was there?"

"Two guns were all I counted shooting. And they got away in the dark. I doubt that I got lead into either one of 'em."

"I'm damned if I know what to say, Marshal. Even if we had a night patrolman, which we're short right now, there wouldn't be much use in sending him out to look for 'em."

"I figured that out myself," Longarm said. "The only thing that I wanta do right now is get rid of that body and the horse it's on, so I can go to the room I got over at the Sampson House and catch up on my shut-eye. I'll come in tomorrow and give you a report."

"Well, then, it looks to me like the best thing to do is for me to lead the nag that fellow's on around in back of the station," the policeman said frowning. "We got a little shed there I can put him in. When Chief Glenn comes on watch, which'll be sometime around six o'clock, I'll tell him about it and he can see to having the undertaker come get the body."

Longarm nodded and told the policeman, "I'll be obliged if you'll do that. And tell Frank I'll be in sometime during the morning to tell him what all happened."

Longarm was still sleeping the following morning when a rapping on the door of his room in the hotel awakened him. He was instantly alert, his hand ready to reach for his Colt hanging in its holster on the back of a chair beside the bed as he called, "Who is it?"

"Dick Bowler, Longarm."

Longarm recognized the Texas Ranger's voice. He slid out of bed and padded to the door, barefoot and in his long johns. He opened the door and looked at Bowler.

"Damned if you fellows here in Texas don't beat all for breaking up a man's sleep," he said. "Well, come on in."

"I figured it was time you oughta be rousted out," Bowler said as they shook hands. "The sun's up and shining and I haven't had breakfast yet. When they told me you were here, I got the idea we might eat together."

"I'd as soon look at you across the table as I would anybody else that grows whiskers," Longarm told him over his shoulder as he slid a cigar out of his vest pocket and flicked a match across his thumbnail. When his cigar was drawing well, he reached for his shirt as he said, "I guess they told you at the police station that I was here."

"Frank Glenn did," Bowler said with a nod. "Said you brought in a good crook last night."

"If he means a dead one, I sure did," Longarm replied. He'd gotten into his trousers by now and was

92

reaching for his boots. "But he was one I didn't finish off. Matter of fact, I was sorry about him dying when he did. There was still a few questions I was figuring to ask him."

"You told the night man at the station that this fellow's name was Scott Coley," Bowler went on. "But you didn't say anything about the ones he was running with."

"If you're talking about Menard and Big Ed Blossom, they're both dead, too."

"Now, I didn't hear Frank say a word about them," Bowler said. "But that Blossom fellow is one son of a bitch I'd like to get my hands on, if you know where he is."

"I sure do. But it won't do you a lot of good, Dick. He's laying out on the prairie, deader'n a doornail."

"Did you and him shoot it out?"

"Me and him and this fellow Menard and the one going under the name of Coley."

"Sounds like it was a right good ruckus."

"Oh, it wasn't much. They didn't have any better sense than to split up when they finally came at me, and gave me a chance at 'em one at a time." By now Longarm was fully dressed. "Come on. I'll tell you the whole story while we're eating breakfast."

"So that's the way it was," Longarm concluded as he and Bowler sat drinking a final cup of after-breakfast coffee in the hotel dining room.

"It's a damn shame you had to shoot that one named Blossom," the Ranger said. "He killed one of us over in Val Verde County almost a year ago, so by rights it ought to've been a Ranger that finished him off."

"Well, I didn't have time to stop and ask him who

else was after him," Longarm replied. "But if you want to ride out with me this morning and bring his body in, I'd be glad to have some company."

"I don't guess you'd mind handing Blossom's body over to me, if I go? It'd maybe mean something on my record up in Austin."

"It won't mean anything to me," Longarm replied. "Sure. If you want to deliver his body, it'll save me trouble."

"I guess I'll ride along, then."

"As long as you're going, you won't mind riding on to Salem with me, I guess," Longarm went on. "Maybe the two of us can make some sense out of the place. That's where my case really is. All this other stuff just sorta happened."

"I had it in mind to ask you about the case that brought you here," Bowler said. "Frank Glenn didn't say much about it."

"It's not rightly a case, Dick," Longarm said. "I was up in Fort Smith where I'd just closed out a case, and Billy Vail wired me to come down here and pick up an old hard-nose they were holding in jail over at Salem. It was that One-finger Carter. You've heard about him, I'd guess?"

"Sure. We been looking for him, too, after we got the word he'd robbed that coach and might be heading down here to Texas."

"Well, it looks like that's just what he did. Anyway, the long and the short of it is that he wound up in that jail in Salem, but when I got there and told 'em I'd come for Carter, they said he was dead."

"Killed?"

"That's the part that got me to stewing. The constable at Salem wouldn't say anything except that Carter had died and they'd buried him."

"It'd be a hell of a note if they'd buried him without looking to make sure he was dead," Bowler said with a smile.

"Stop joshing me, Dick," Longarm protested smilingly. "I had to waste a lot of time waiting for the doctor to make me out a death certificate for Carter, then when I started back here them three outlaws began chasing me. I found a way to stand 'em off, shot two of 'em, and put the cuffs on this Coley fellow. And then somebody bushwhacked us just when we were leaving the railroad yard and killed Coley."

"What I can't figure out is why you didn't bring the other two outlaws' bodies with you when you headed back to Waco," Bowler said. "That's what I'd've done."

"On account of Coley'd got shot up pretty bad and I needed to get him to a doctor. I didn't have time to waste rounding up them dead fellows' horses and loading 'em onto the nags."

"I guess I'd've done the same thing," Bowler acknowledged. He looked at their emptied plates and cups and went on, "I don't know about you, but I'm finished eating. Now, I've got to go back to the police station and tell Frank Glenn where I'll be in case I get a wire from Austin. You figure you can be saddled up by the time I get back?"

"Sure. If we get started now. I'll be ready when you get back. Just come to the stable in back of the hotel."

Longarm was waiting at the stable, his saddlebags checked, his horse saddled and ready, when Dick Bowler returned. As soon as he saw Longarm, the Ranger began shaking his head. When he reined in, he said, "I hate not to do what I said I'd do, Longarm, but I can't go with you."

"You mean you got sent out on another case before you closed the one that got you here?"

"That's right. And it might be a big one. There was a wire from Ranger Headquarters waiting for me when I got to the police station. It seems that somebody in a little two-bit town about a day's ride from here called Smiley thought they saw John Wesley Hardin get off a train there. I've got to go make sure. He's still wanted for breaking out of the pen, you know."

"I seem to recall that he is," Longarm said. "And he's a lot bigger game than these fellows I tangled with. Well, we'll run into each other someplace else. You take care of Hardin, if it's him, and I'll go settle my own case."

Longarm replied to Bowler's wave as the Ranger rode off. Then he swung into the saddle of his own horse and started for the now-familiar trail that led to Salem.

# Chapter 8

Off the trail just ahead of him Longarm saw the low hillock where the trio had jumped him the day before— and had paid with their lives for their attempt to murder him. He turned the livery horse toward the hump and let it pick its own way up the slope, touching the reins only occasionally to keep it in a straight path.

As the horse drew closer to the top of the rise a frown grew on Longarm's face. By now he'd expected to see the horses ridden by the dead men. Between the huisache patches that dotted the sloping sides of the rise there was plenty of graze to have kept a dozen horses satisfied overnight, and even where the shrubs grew thickest they did not rise high enough to hide the back of a horse.

Longarm had anticipated that the dead outlaws' horses would stray a short distance as they browsed during the night, but he hadn't expected them to have vanished completely. He scanned as much of the slope as he could see in his approach, and when he reached the crest of the hump, rode across it and looked down the side which had been hidden on his approach. The animals were not on that slope, either, and the shortgrass that predominated on the prairie did not grow tall enough to conceal a gopher or a prairie dog, to say nothing of a horse.

Dismounting, Longarm started walking back and forth around the clumps of huisache. Their growth was both thick enough and high enough to hide a body. As he looked, he reconstructed the previous day's gunfight in his memory. That his recollection was good got quick confirmation. When he reached the spot where he'd seen Menard fall, the undergrowth still had not sprung back into place and the ground at the roots of the hui-sache clumps bore the stains of blood that had blackened overnight.

Stepping to the place where he'd bandaged Coley there were still a few threads of the shirtsleeve he'd ripped apart, as well as traces of dried blood where the gunman had fallen. He moved to the area where he'd dropped Pinkie, or Blossom, as he'd later learned. There, too, the light-tan soil showed dark crusted spots where the third gunman had dropped.

"Now look here, old son," Longarm admonished himself as he gazed at the stained ground. "Dead men don't just get up and walk away, and them two fellows yesterday were about as dead as anybody's ever going to be."

Walking to the far side of the slope he found the spot where he'd stretched out and used the huisache for cover. The glint of the cartridge cases he'd discarded when reloading caught his eyes at once, and when he looked back across the humped top of the hillock, the evidence once again confirmed his recollection of the brief gunfight.

"So there ain't but one thing that could've happened," Longarm said into the empty air while his fingers moved as of their own volition to take a cigar from his pocket. "Somebody took the bodies and the horses away during the night, or maybe earlier this morning." He flicked a match into flame and lit the stogie while his thoughts continued to flow. "Now, that somebody—likely more than one of 'em—just about had to come from Salem. And whoever it was that moved the bodies must've carried 'em back there to keep from having to answer a lot of questions later on."

Satisfied that he'd reached the only possible conclusion, Longarm remounted and rode down the side of the hump, where he turned his horse in the direction of Salem.

Although the day was well along by the time he reached the little hamlet, there were no workers in the fields of the farms that he passed as he approached the town, and no smoke rose from the farmhouse chimneys. Salem itself still looked half-asleep when he reached it. The road, or street, that meandered through the village was deserted. Shuttered windows greeted his eyes at each of the widely separated houses he passed. The store where he'd gotten such scant welcome on his earlier visit was closed.

"Looks like everybody just up and moved away," Longarm muttered as he came to the doctor's house.

It was also shuttered, but he reined in anyhow and dismounted, then walked slowly to the door. He knocked and waited. When the door was not opened he knocked again. This time he tapped his knuckles on the panel with more force and prolonged his rapping. He'd waited for several minutes and was about to turn away when the door opened. Ellie stood there.

"Why, Marshal Long!" she exclaimed. "You're the last one I expected to see! Do come in."

As he stepped inside, Longarm said, "I'm looking for your daddy, Ellie. Is he at home?"

She shook her head. "No. He'd already left when I got up this morning. Unless—" She paused, frowning, then went on, "Unless he got called out in the night."

They'd reached the parlor now. Ellie motioned toward a chair, and as Longarm sat down he asked, "But when he goes out at night, don't he tap on your door and tell you where he's going, and maybe how long he'll be gone, so you won't be worrying?"

"Not always. But I, well, I don't worry anymore about not knowing where Father is, Marshal. I'm used to folks coming for him at all hours."

"That figures," Longarm said. "Him being the only doctor and all like that."

Ellie went on, "Most of the time I wake up when somebody comes after him in the middle of the night, or he'll wake me up, like I just told you."

"And if you don't know where he went or anything, you don't ever know when to look for him back," Longarm said. "Well, I guess the thing for me to do is go on out and talk to the constable. I have to see him, too, while I'm here."

"I'm sure you'll find him at home," Ellie said. "He doesn't have a wife, you know, so he's likely to be fixing his meal about this time."

"I guess I haven't been paying much attention to what time it's got to be. Guess I better dig my rations outa my saddlebags and have a bite while I'm riding out there."

"You can't eat a decent meal on horseback, Marshal Long!"

"Oh, I manage to get by."

"I won't hear of you doing such a thing! I've cooked up a good meal for Papa and me, and there's more than enough for you, too. It's not anything fancy, just stew and apple pie, but it's ready to eat. So if you'll just give me a minute to dish some up, we'll sit down and—"

"Hold on, Miss Ellie! What about the doctor?"

"He's used to me keeping his meals hot for him to have whenever he manages to get home. If he's not here, I'll just have a bite by myself. You'll be doing me a favor by sitting down and keeping me company, Marshal."

"Well, now, when you put it that way, I sure find it hard to say no. I'll be right proud to join you."

Though the meal served by Ellie was far from being fancy, her Irish stew was flavorful and filling, and the slice of pie made from sun-dried apples was more than satisfying. Longarm felt well fed when he finished the last bite of pie and drained his coffee cup. He slid a cigar from his pocket and lit it, then rose and made a half bow toward Ellie.

"That was sure fine, and I thank you kindly for inviting me. But if I'm going to get my job done today, I have to get on out to the constable's now, and see if I can finish up my business with him."

"I guess you'll be stopping by here to see Father, on your way back to Waco?" Ellie asked. "Or do you want me to tell him something?"

Longarm hesitated for a moment, then said, "I don't guess him being out had anything to do with them two dead men I left on a little hill between here and Waco? Or that you'd know anything about 'em?"

"Dead men? You mean there's been some trouble?"

"A little bit. It's all past and over with now, so there's not anything for you to fret about."

"Well, my goodness!" she exclaimed. "This is the first I've heard about it! What happened?"

"Why, there were some fellows after me when I started back to Waco yesterday evening. They started shooting and I shot back, and the shooting wound up with two of 'em dead and the other one hurt, so I took him on into Waco with me. And this morning I came out from Waco to see about the dead ones, but their bodies weren't there. That's what I've come back to Salem for, to find out whatever I can about the other two."

"But Perc Moore would know more about that than Father," she said. "I don't guess you've talked to him yet, though."

"I just rode in, but that's where I'm going now. When I was passing your house here it came to my mind that your daddy being the coroner, he might know some things that'd help me. But it ain't something for you to worry about, Ellie." Longarm added, "I'll go on out and see the constable. If I need to ask your daddy any questions, I'll stop on my way back."

"You do that, Marshal Long," she said. "And I'll tell him you might stop, so he'll be sure to be here."

Percival Moore's house, standing alone and away from town as it did, with its shutters drawn and its doors closed, looked deserted as Longarm rode up. Then he saw that the door of the storm-cellar-turned-jail was propped open and decided that Moore might be inside it. He toed his horse over to the slanted semicircular door and dismounted.

This was the first time he'd been close enough to the semisubterranean structure to see any of its construction details. The doors were made from thick wooden planks and their form reminded Longarm of church doors with their arched tops. These doors were much shorter, however. They opened in the center of a red-brick arch that slanted behind them to ground level and disappeared beneath the ground.

Now the doors were both open, and Longarm peered down the steps that led from the red bricks of the sunken threshold into the dim recesses of what seemed to Longarm to be a single big room. He descended two of the six steps and bent down to look into the gloom of the underground chamber.

As its outer formation had suggested, it was an arched vaultlike enclosure, and was much larger than had been suggested by its entranceway. Longarm guessed that the domed circular room was a least fifteen or perhaps twenty feet in diameter. When he took out a match and scraped his thumbnail across its head, the faint light that it gave illuminated the vaultlike space only dimly. He could make out a table and two or three chairs standing in the recess formed by its back wall, two small cotlike single beds in the arc of its side walls, and a large rolltop desk in the curve behind the stairs.

Longarm went on down the steps to the floor of the room. His match had burned to a short stub now, so he let it fall to the brick floor and struck another. A section of stovepipe hanging from the wall at the back caught his eye by the shadow it cast on the wall behind it; he guessed that it must be some sort of elbowed air vent, for no light came through its bottom. He looked for other furniture, a table that might hold a lamp or a lantern or candlestick, but saw none.

"Well, you got to say one thing about this place, old son," he told himself. "That constable's no slouch when it comes to fixing a real solid lockup. If a fellow was to be tucked away in here he'd sure have one hell of a job busting out, with that thick heavy door and no kind of a window to work on."

He gave the room a second sweeping glance before the match began to burn his fingers, then blew it out as he turned and started up the steps. Blinking as he emerged into the bright afternoon sunlight, he turned to peer one last time into the entrance of the underground chamber, then looked toward the constable's house, but saw no sign that Moore had returned.

Mounting his horse, Longarm started back toward Salem. He'd ridden only a hundred yards or so when he glanced over his shoulder. Percy Moore, a lantern in one hand, was emerging from the storm cellar that had been totally deserted less than five minutes ago.

For a moment Longarm did not quite believe his eyes. He blinked once, then again, before returning his gaze to Moore. His mind was working at top speed while he watched the Salem constable. Moore still stood on the steps of the storm cellar. He was bending forward to blow out the lantern he carried, and it was obvious he wasn't aware that Longarm was anywhere near.

Longarm wheeled his horse and started back to the cellar's entrance before Moore looked up when he heard hoofbeats. His face held a surprised look, but he'd managed to regain his composure by the time Longarm reined up in front of him.

"Well, howdy, Marshal Long," he said as Longarm pulled his horse up. His voice sounded something less than cheerful when he went on, "What brings you out here again today? I figured you'd be on your way back up to Denver by now."

"Oh, I put off going back for a spell." Longarm kept his tone carefully casual. "There's two or three loose ends I got to tie up."

"You mean your case wasn't closed when you found out that fellow you were looking for was dead?"

"It seems like that case has led me right into another one," Longarm told Moore. "I ain't sure yet whether they're connected up some way. That's what I aim to find out."

Moore shook his head. His face was without any expression at all, but his voice carried a small nervous edge when he asked, "How'd they be connected?"

"One way is that there's more'n one dead crook now." When Longarm's reply brought the tiniest flicker of a frown over the constable's face he went on. "You see, Constable, I had a little run-in on my way back to Waco."

"Run-in with who?" Moore frowned.

"Three fellows. One of 'em was named Menard, he traveled under the name of Mannie sometimes. Another one was Big Ed Blossom—" Longarm stopped when he saw the constable's reaction to Blossom's name and the effort the old man was making to hide it, then went on. "They wanted a shoot-out, and I couldn't do much but oblige 'em."

"But I see you walked away from it," Moore said. "How did they come out of it?"

"I shot and killed both of them, out on the little hill on the prairie between here and Waco. I guess you'd know the place I'm talking about?"

"I, well, I know there's a sorta rise, but it wouldn't rate much as a hill."

"I figure it's the closest thing to a hill between here and Waco, so you'd be pretty sure to know where I'm talking about."

"I, I guess I do," Moore admitted a bit reluctantly.

"Like I said, I brought down them two, but I'd put a hole in the other one while we were swapping lead. I had to leave them dead men laying there while I took the one that was shot into Waco, to find a doctor."

"So he's all right, then?" the constable asked.

"Not so's you'd notice. When we got to Waco there were some outa the bunch that'd made it there ahead of us. They were right outside the railroad yards, waiting

105

for us. I hadn't counted on that. They bushwhacked us, got off the first shots and killed him."

"Then you don't know why the three of 'em were coming after you?" Moore tried to suppress the breath of relief that went with his question, but Longarm's sharply attuned ears caught its overtones.

"Not for sure, I don't," Longarm went on. "But there's more to it that I haven't told you yet."

"I don't see what else could've happened, but go ahead and finish."

"There wasn't much use in me going back out to the prairie to bring in the bodies of them other two outlaws that I'd had to leave," Longarm went on. "So I waited till this morning. And do you know what? Them two outlaws' bodies were gone when I got back there."

"Somebody must've run across them, and carried them into Waco," Moore suggested.

"Not likely. They weren't laying anywhere near the trail."

"What do you suppose happened to them, then?"

"I sorta got the idea that maybe it was somebody from Salem that found 'em and brought 'em back here. That's why I came out here looking for you. If them bodies were brought here, you'd be the one to know about it."

Moore shook his head. "I'd've told you before now if there'd been anything like that happen."

"It looks like I've got a real puzzle on my hands, then," Longarm said, shaking his head. "But I'll get to the bottom of it, sooner or later."

"I suppose so," the constable said nodding. "But right now, my throat's dry as dust, standing out here in the sun talking. Your gullet's bound to be like mine is. Why don't we go over to my little old house? I'll pour

106

us a glass of some good New England cider they make out of apples that grows back home."

"Now that's a real thoughtful invitation," Longarm said. "And I'll be glad to take you up on it. But as long as we're standing here so close, before we go over to your house, I'd sorta like to see this storm cellar you've turned into your jail."

"Now, there ain't really all that much to see," Moore replied quickly. "I seem to recall telling you I didn't put no bars up, or anything fancy like that."

"So you did. But since I've been wearing a lawman's badge, I've seen a lot of jails here and there across the country, and I never did see one in a storm cellar before. I've been downright curious to see how this one of yours works out."

"Like I said, there's not a thing to see down there. Just the walls and a couple of cots and a few sticks of furniture. I don't see that there'd be much you'd be interested in."

"Why, I've already told you why I'd like to look at it. It won't take us but a minute to light your lantern and step down them stairs behind you."

"Well . . ."

Both Moore's words and his tone had carried the overtones of his reluctance until now. Longarm was quicker than most in reading a message in the tone of a person's voice, and he was aware of the constable's surrender with that single reluctant word. Before Moore could go on, Longarm had slipped a match from his vest pocket and was bending down to lift the lantern's chimney and touch the wick before Moore could say anything else.

As he straightened up, Longarm said, "You lead the

way, you know better'n I do about them steps and such."

Holding the lantern as high as the brick arch above the steps allowed him to, the constable started down the stairs. Longarm followed him closely. Moore stopped at the foot of the short flight and said, "Now look out for your head, Marshal Long. You're a mite taller than me or most of the prisoners that I bring down here."

With the lantern's glow filling the round, domed chamber, Longarm could now see plainly what had been shadowed before. In the light, the circular room displayed its actual size, which had been hidden by shadows on his previous and quickly curtailed inspection. Reflected from the light-red bricks from which the walls had been made, the chamber had a rosy hue, even in the yellowish lanternlight. Longarm made a show of surprise that was feigned little more than his genuine astonishment earlier.

"How'd you come by all these fine fancy bricks?" he asked as he started around the room's perimeter, running the palm of one hand along the wall. "I don't recall seeing any exactly like 'em before now."

"Oh, some fellow in Waco had them made special and shipped out here for a house he was going to put up. But the bricks took so long getting here that his house was already finished, and I bought 'em off him."

Longarm had covered about half the cellar's wall now, and still hadn't found what he was sure must exist: the telltale seams that would give away the location of a hidden door. Though he had no idea what such a door would hide or into what fresh maze it might lead, he knew that any further delay might endanger his investigation, for Moore was having trouble hiding his impatience.

"Well, I guess I've seen enough," Longarm told the constable. "You sure got a fancy little jail here, I'll give you credit for that. But I'm about ready now to go sample that cider you said you'd pour."

"And I meant it, too," Moore said. He started toward the cellar door, looking back anxiously to be sure Longarm was following him.

Outside, the day was waning fast. Moore led the way to his house, and as they drew close to the shuttered dwelling, he turned and said loudly, "My little house isn't much for fancy, Marshal Long, but it's cool and comfortable inside. We'll have a glass or two of cider, and maybe things will look better to you then."

"They might at that," Longarm agreed. "Because I don't mind telling you, just as one lawman to the next one, I sure don't have any leads to follow right this minute. That don't mean I'm giving up, you understand. I don't take kindly to losing prisoners, or having 'em killed while I'm responsible for 'em. I'll pick up a trail somewhere along the way, and I aim to follow it as long and as far as I have to till I get to the end of it!"

# Chapter 9

"Well, that sure does you credit, Marshal Long," Moore said as he unlocked the door of his house and threw it open. "It ain't everybody that'd stick to a job the way you're doing. Now, just step right on in the house. We'll have a comfortable place to sit down there."

Longarm frowned as he responded to the constable's invitation. He was sure he'd heard noises coming from the house before the door opened, but now there was only silence in the cool air that trickled onto the steps. When he entered he found that the room he was in was almost as cool inside as the cellar had been. The blinds at the windows were closed, giving the room a twilight atmosphere.

"I got to admit, this sure is a lot better'n that hot sun outdoors," Longarm remarked. "It's funny, but I ain't seen many houses up in this part of Texas that's got window blinds. Seems like there oughta be more."

"Most of the houses here in Salem have them," Moore said. "I guess that's because all of us here came from the real Salem, the old one back in New England. All the houses there are fixed up this way, and I guess having blinds here sort of reminds us of home. Now, sit down and rest while I go out to the kitchen and fetch the cider jug."

After the constable crossed to a door on the opposite side of the room and disappeared through it, Longarm took stock of his surroundings. In some ways the sparsely furnished chamber reminded him of the doctor's house. It had the same kind of faded Oriental rug on the floor, the furniture was angular and looked uncomfortable, and the three pictures that decorated its walls were of seashore scenes.

He selected an armchair and sat down a bit gingerly, then found that for all its squareness the chair was surprisingly comfortable. He was just getting settled when Moore returned, carrying an earthenware jug and two teacups.

"I think you'll find this cider tasty," he told Longarm. "I get a half dozen jugs from back home every year right after apple harvest, and they don't last but a little while."

"I never did work up a taste for cider," Longarm remarked as he took the cup his host handed him and held it under the mouth of the jug the constable had uncorked. "But I guess that's because down in West Virginia where I grew up there wasn't nobody that could get apple trees to take good root."

"It takes a lot of rain to grow trees. I suppose that's why there was an apple tree or two in just about everybody's yard, back in Old Salem," Moore said. He held up his cup and went on, "Don't wait for me to give you a toast, Marshal. Just drink the cider and enjoy it."

Longarm took a healthy swallow of the sweet-smelling cider. He discovered that it was not as sweet as its aroma had promised, but had a tarty tang that called for another swallow and another after that.

"That's a right nice little tipple," he told Moore, taking his cup from his lips.

"Glad you like it, Marshal," Moore said. "Drink it down. There's plenty more in the jug."

Longarm swallowed another mouthful of the cider. As he took a cheroot from his pocket, he said, "Yessir. This stuff ain't too sweet and it ain't too tarty. Of course, it ain't got the edgy bite that a fellow gets out of a shot of good whiskey, but a man could get to like it, all the same."

Moore had placed the jug on the floor beside his chair. He picked it up and held it out to Longarm. "Fill up whenever you've got a notion to," he invited. "Like they say back home, a man can't walk on just one leg."

"I'll just light up my cigar, then I'll finish the swallow or two I still got here before I pour again," Longarm replied. He took a match from his vest pocket and scratched his horny thumbnail across its head. It flared into flame and he puffed his stogie until it was drawing to suit him. Then he swallowed another large mouthful of the cider. As he brought the cup down from his lips he looked at his host.

"How come you're not drinking yours?" he asked.

"I am," Moore replied. "I guess you just didn't notice."

"Well, since you've invited me, I'll pour another little swallow." Longarm picked up the jug. In order to have a hand free to pull the cork, he placed his cup on the floor beside his chair. He pulled the cork out and was reaching for his cup when his hand stopped, poised halfway to the floor.

"Damned if this cider ain't got more authority than I figured," he said, shaking his head. "I guess I better ride on what I've already drunk."

"You're just imagining things," Moore said. "You've got a better head for liquor than that."

"I ain't so sure," Longarm replied, shaking his head from side to side. "I got a sorta funny feeling, like I was . . ." He swallowed hard and went on, "Now, I sure as sin ain't getting . . ." He stopped again and began opening and closing his mouth as though he were tasting some kind of new dish.

"Damn you, Moore!" he exclaimed, his chest heaving as he found himself unable to draw fresh air into his lungs. "You put something in this—" Longarm stopped abruptly. The jug dropped to the floor. Then he toppled from his chair and lay sprawled beside it, his eyes closed, knowing nothing more.

For some time Longarm had been hearing sounds, but his mind was only partially functioning. Although he'd been aware for several minutes of the noises that were reaching him, his mind had not registered them as words which signified that somewhere close by, men were speaking.

By the time he'd started to understand what he was hearing, and the sounds that had been only meaningless babble were reaching him as words, Longarm's mind was beginning to return to its customary incisiveness. Now, as the foggy darkness that had numbed his senses began to lift and clear away, he could link the words into sentences that had a meaning.

". . . have enough here to make a coven," were the first words Longarm heard plainly.

He did not recognize the voice, nor did he understand what the speaker meant. He wanted to ask the man, "What's a coven, anyway?"

"Tomorrow night the moon will be right for an *esbat*," another man said.

Again, the rough graveled voice Longarm heard was strange to him, and he did not know the meaning of *esbat*.

"Even if it is, Morsund, the calendar is not right for a sabbat," a third man chimed in.

*Sabbat* was another word outside of Longarm's understanding, but he found himself wondering if the speaker could have been saying *Sabbath,* and he'd misunderstood because of the fog that still hung on in his mind and blocked his memory.

Now a voice that Longarm recognized broke into the silence which had fallen. It was Percy Moore's voice.

"Nothing any of you said is important," the constable was saying. "We should ask our Speaker what she wants to do. If she doesn't know, she will get the true answer by casting the *athame.*"

Longarm shook his head. Nothing that he'd heard so far made a bit of sense to him. He'd come out of the strange darkness that had seized him so suddenly with fog still clouding his mind, but his years of experience as a lawman had developed his instinct to survive.

He'd been lying motionless while his mind cleared, still unsure of anything except that voices were reaching his ears. Even after he'd begun to hear them, the strange words spoken by the first two men had started him to wondering why he was on the floor. Almost at once Longarm's silent internal inquiry moved to the question of how he'd gotten there.

This question had stumped him for a few moments after he'd begun pondering it. Only after he'd carried on his inner debate for several moments after finding the answer to his initial questions did he accept the fact that for no reason he could think of, he was stretched out in darkness in some unknown place. His mind seemed to be working with unusual sluggishness, and Longarm started to question whether he was dreaming, or whether he was awake and listening to some unfamiliar kind of drunken gibberish.

However, the fog that had clouded Longarm's brain

was beginning to lift now. In the beginning its dissolution was slow, and more than a little painful. After hearing the first voice that he'd recognized, his mind had started working a bit faster, but it still held blank areas where memory failed him. He still did not understand why his limbs refused to obey him, or why his hands and feet felt cold and numb.

Above all, he wondered why he was unable to see anything, now that his eyes were open. He tried to peer through the darkness, but lying as he was, on his side, still unable to lift his head from the cold floor, all that he saw in front of him was blackness. Now the voices began again and Longarm stopped wondering in order to listen.

"Shall we take him to the Speaker, then?" asked the man who'd started the conversation.

"Of course we must, Clete," Moore said. "Our bond is made to her."

"Belthane must be the judge," another of the unseen speakers agreed.

"Then there's no reason for us to sit here and talk any longer," Moore told his companions. "Let's take him to her."

Longarm heard the sounds of movement and by this time he'd recovered enough to understand that the speakers to whom he'd been listening with such puzzlement were moving. He decided at once that his best bet was to let them think he was still unconscious. He closed his eyes and let his muscles go limp.

Now the sound of booted feet thunking on the stone floor reached his ears. The footsteps drew closer, and he realized that the men who'd been talking had been very close to him. The footsteps stopped.

"He's still asleep," one of them said. "You must have made the draught very potent."

"Marshal Long is a big healthy man," Moore replied. "To be safe, I put in almost double the usual dose."

"How long will he be unconscious?" another asked.

"It's hard to say," Moore told the questioner. "But long enough for us to carry him to Belthane. Pick him up and let's get started."

"Sure." The man who'd spoken was not one whose voice Longarm had heard before. He went on, "I'll carry the lantern."

Longarm was careful to keep his eyes closed and his muscles totally relaxed as hands grasped his upper arms and his feet and lifted him from the stone floor. When they raised him, he discovered that not only were his arms pulled behind his back and his wrists secured by his own handcuffs, but that his ankles had also been lashed together. The man at his head had little trouble raising him from the floor as he simply thrust his hands into Longarm's armpits. But the man at his feet groped and pawed for several moments before he succeeded in getting a hand on the ropes holding his ankles together.

Then Longarm was swaying in midair, his head dropped backward, the tendons and muscles in his neck stretched uncomfortably taut. His handcuffs were cutting into his wrists and the rope around his ankles bit into them painfully as the men began carrying him and Longarm's body swayed. His backward-lolling head put an unaccustomed strain on his neck and shoulder muscles and they quickly began aching, but he resisted the temptation to open his eyes and to shift his pinioned hands.

Now all that Longarm could hear were feet thunking crisply on the stone floor and the rustle of the clothing

116

worn by the men who were carrying him. As the minutes stretched out he became able to distinguish some of the sounds and isolate them and identify them.

In addition to the four men who carried him like a bag of onions or potatoes, there were at least two others. They said nothing as they moved, so he was unable to determine whether Moore was one of the four who were carrying him, or one of the pair walking ahead of and behind him.

At least, he told himself silently as his head continued to clear in spite of—or perhaps because of—its swaying, he knew now that there were six of them. From the lack of weight in his cross-draw holster, he knew also that he was without his Colt. Longarm wondered if his captors had searched him beyond taking the gun while he'd been unconscious. His mind would have been much easier if he'd been able to feel for and find that he still had the little backup derringer that he kept in his vest pocket.

Then he thought of his handcuff key, which, since the near-escape of Cal Peters in New Mexico a few years ago, he'd begun carrying in a narrow pocket of suede leather sewn into the upper edge of his left boot. There was no way that he could feel for the key under his present circumstances, but he was reasonably sure that when his captors had handcuffed him, they'd been more concerned with placing the manacles on his wrists than in thinking about the key that would release them.

A strange odor, one which he was unable to identify, suddenly reached Longarm's nose and diverted his attention from the problems he was mulling over. It had nothing in common with any of the scents with which he was familiar. The smell was pungent without being acrid, sweet without being cloying, and it somehow

117

managed to be both pleasant and unpleasant at the same time.

After he'd been aware of the alien aroma for a few moments, Longarm suddenly remembered where he'd smelled a similar scent once before. That had been in San Francisco, when the case that he was working at the time had taken him to Chinatown, and now he knew that the alien odor must be some kind of incense.

He was just beginning to resume his efforts to plan some kind of move leading to his escape when the men carrying him dumped him unceremoniously on the hard stone floor. Being dropped so unexpectedly almost brought an involuntary grunt from Longarm, but he caught it in time to stop it while it was still an almost inaudible gurgle in his throat.

Then Moore's voice broke the silence which the men carrying Longarm had maintained since they began moving, and for the first time Longarm had reached the state of alertness that enabled him to realize he was in trouble.

"Leave him here," the constable said, "Belthane will come out soon. She knows that we're waiting for her."

Longarm wondered when he heard Moore's assured tone just how the mysterious Belthane would know, but the thought had just entered his mind when light footsteps reached his ears and a woman's voice broke the silence.

"Have you brought me a pretty new toy, now?" she asked. Her voice was low, deep and throaty, and she spoke little louder than a whisper.

"A new one, yes," Moore replied.

"He looks dead," the woman said.

"It's only because the potion hasn't worked off yet,"

Moore assured her. "There's not been enough time for him to recover."

"Will he be asleep much longer, then?"

"A little while."

"Then am I to have him for myself until we celebrate the next sabbat?" she asked.

Longarm's curiosity was growing with each exchange between the woman and the constable. The temptation to slit his eyes and look at her was almost overpowering, for her voice had a haunting familiarity that he'd been trying to place almost from the first moment he'd heard her speak. He resisted the temptation, and kept his eyes closed.

Almost before Belthane's voice had died away, one of the men said, "It's not time for a sabbat."

Longarm recognized the gravel-rough voice of the objector, and it was a voice to which he could attach a name. It was Morsund, the same man who'd objected on the same matter when the group had been discussing his fate earlier.

"Time or no time, I say we should have one."

This voice belonged to another of those making up the group to whom Longarm could give a name, Clete. Clete was the other of the two men who'd spoken earlier, and to whom Moore had replied by name. At the time he'd heard their names, Longarm had progressed far enough toward recovering to have tucked both names into his memory without having realized that he was doing so.

Belthane replied firmly to Clete, saying, "We will not talk now about a sabbat. I will decide later whether we shall have one."

Now Moore broke in, his voice submissive. "Whatever you wish, Belthane."

119

"I wish you to leave me now," Belthane said.

"Aren't you hungry?" Moore asked.

"No. When I want you again, I will call you. Then you must bring me some food," she answered.

"You've all heard Belthane speak," Moore said. "We'll go back to the house and wait until she calls for us."

"But what about him?" one of the men asked.

His voice was one that Longarm did not yet associate with a name, but Moore filled in that vacant spot.

"He's like all the others, Barton," the constable said. "He belongs to Belthane until she returns him to us."

"Sure," Barton mumbled. "I know. It's only when we don't bring her somebody new for a good long spell that she's got any time for us."

"That's as it should be," Moore replied. "Come on, let's get on back. I don't know about the rest of you, but I've still got chores left to do today."

Longarm listened to the noises made by the men as they left. When the thunking of their feet on the stone floor died away, leaving him alone with the woman, he finally opened his eyes and stirred. Belthane, the woman whose voice he'd heard but who he hadn't seen clearly before, was standing beside him.

At first he saw her only as a figure silhouetted against the wavering flame from a single fat candle that rose behind her in a candelabrum as tall as a man's shoulders. She studied him for a moment, then bent forward to examine his face more closely. By now Longarm's eyes had adjusted to the dim candlelight that eased the gloom of the big stone-lined chamber and at the same time emphasized it. His eyes widened as he looked at Belthane and his jaw dropped as he began to make out her features.

120

For a moment he stared without believing the evidence of his eyes. Belthane's cheekbones were high, her nose short and straight. She had over-full lips, now pursed into a thoughtful pout that made them seem even fuller. Her chin was firm and blunt, almost squared. Except for the fluffy tousled mass of dark curling hair that flared out and covered her ears and cascaded in a welter of tangles below her shoulders, Longarm realized that while he knew this woman's name to be Belthane, he might well be looking at Ellie.

Only a few features kept the resemblance between the two from being short of perfection. Belthane's eyes were midnight black, Ellie's eyes were a bright blue. Ellie's cheeks were rounded, her face fleshed out, and her skin had a healthy roseate glow. Her lips were thinner than Belthane's, which protruded as though she were pouting over some real or fancied slight. The noses of both followed the same lines, straight from brow to tip, with flared nostrils, but Belthane's nostrils seemed thicker and perhaps a bit wider.

While both women had the same high cheekbones, in Belthane's thinner face these seemed to be higher and more prominent. Her chin was sharper than Ellie's and in the yellowish candlelight her skin had a uniform waxen pallor. Belthane's clothing bore no resemblance to the gingham dresses with wide, stiffly starched and shining white cuffs and collars that were all Longarm had seen Ellie wear.

Belthane had on a dark flowing robe of midnight-black which had a spreading collar that was equally black. The robe had long sleeves and no touch of white relieved its somber hue, though Longarm caught a glimpse of a gold necklace that supported a device which looked like a key, also of gold. In spite of the differences between the two young women, Longarm could see Ellie in Belthane and Belthane in Ellie.

Until now Longarm had remained silent, and Belthane had said nothing during the moments she'd spent examining him. Now he asked, "You're Ellie's older sister, aren't you?"

Belthane stayed silent—she seemed to be debating with herself whether to answer his question or ignore it. When she saw Longarm's lips twitch as a preliminary to repeating his query, she said at last, "I claim sisterhood only with adepts of the Craft, and only those of the Craft are allowed to sisterhood with me."

"Just what kinda craft is it you're talking about?" Longarm asked.

"You must know, now that you have seen me."

"Whether I do or don't, I'd rather have you tell me yourself," Longarm replied. "That way I'm not likely to make no mistakes."

"Surely you have heard of the ancient craft created by Ianus, who fathered the Triple Goddess," Belthane said.

"It sounds to me like this Ianus fellow's some kind of foreigner," Longarm said frowning. "And I'm still not right sure what kinda craft it is you keep talking about."

"Then you shall learn," Belthane told him. "And I will be your teacher. Think of that, mortal man! Think of it while I prepare to teach you!"

# Chapter 10

"It don't look to me like I got much of a say-so, laying here thrown and hog-tied like I am," Longarm said. "Maybe if you was to let me go——"

"Be quiet, mortal!" Belthane commanded. "I must make sure that the auspices are favorable before we begin!"

From some hidden sheath concealed by the folds of her skirt, she suddenly produced a knife such as Longarm had never seen before. The weapon had a long pointed blade, but instead of the line of the wicked, glinting sliver of steel being smoothly tapered, the blade had a shallow U-shaped jog near the hilt.

Bending over Longarm, Belthane slowly lowered the tip of the strange crooked blade until it rested on his throat. Though the point that Longarm felt was needle-sharp, he did not flinch, and his eyes remained fixed on hers.

"There ain't no way I can stop you from pushing that right on through my guzzle," he told her. Then, keeping his voice low and level, he went on, "But if you got in mind what I figure you have, I ain't going to be much use to you if you start poking holes into me."

"Do not interrupt me again, or you will live only long enough to regret your foolishness!" Belthane warned him. "The Ancient Ones will be glad if I send you to them, but if I find that you please me, I may keep you with me for a while."

Longarm was well aware that he'd pushed as far as

was wise. He said nothing, but nodded, and Belthane lifted the knife tip from his throat.

In spite of the light pressure she'd used while she was holding her weapon to Longarm's bare skin, the tip of the blade carried a small drop of blood with it when she brought it up. Belthane glanced at the shimmering red drop, then returning her gaze to Longarm and keeping their eyes locked, she lifted the knife to her mouth. Her tongue darted out and licked away the blood, then she pursed her full red lips into a budded smile.

Longarm had seen evil in human eyes before, but that which was carried by Belthane's glance was more sinister and foreboding than any he'd yet encountered. When she smiled at him after their stare had lasted a full minute, the line of her lips changed, but not the look in her eyes.

"You are a strong one!" she exclaimed. "You will give me great pleasure! Now stay quiet until I finish my rites and am ready to begin!"

Longarm did not reply. He lay motionless, his mind busy trying to work out a way to reach the key to his handcuffs, his eyes fixed on Belthane. She'd begun a sort of whirling dance without music, whirling to some rhythm that she heard in her imagination. Her head was thrown back and her tousle of hair streamed and tossed as she twirled. Her moves and gestures seemed to have no point, no start, no ending. As she turned and swayed she stepped out of the low-cut sandals she'd been wearing, then started to twirl while remaining in a single spot at Longarm's feet.

Her head was no longer thrown back, but now she'd squeezed her eyes tightly closed and her full lips were parted, moving as she silently mouthed some sort of silent chant or song to a rhythm that existed only in her mind. Now and then her tongue darted out to lick her lips, and when she did this they glistened blood-red for several moments in the candlelight. The glints from Belthane's eyes were as metallically hard as were those from the blade of the oddly shaped dagger with which she'd threatened Longarm. Its bright blade was also sending small darts of brightness around her when her arms moved.

As Belthane's gyrations grew wilder she began humming a low broken buzz that seemed to Longarm to come from deep inside her body rather than from her throat. After she'd been dancing for several minutes her free hand went to the high neck of her long flowing dress. She fumbled with its buttons for a moment then stood motionless while she let the dress slide down her body.

As the garment dropped into a wrinkled heap on the stone floor, Belthane stood as motionless as a statue. Her arms were stretched high now. The dagger in her hand caught the candlelight in darts of dancing flashes, and the long gold necklace which was swaying gently over her full breasts made a shining moving vee as it moved from side to side. The tip of the vee, where the medallion hung only a few inches above the glistening black of her pubic brush, seemed to be an arrow pointing to her ultimate femininity.

Longarm was not aroused by Belthane's nakedness. His mind was too busy, for while she danced he'd prodded his brain trying to think of a way to free himself. During the moments when Belthane was pirouetting, her attention divided between him and the silent music, Longarm had tested his bonds again.

He'd found the handcuffs impossible to shift with the limited leverage allowed his fingers, but he'd gotten a bit of encouragement when he stressed the coils that pulled his feet together. During the time he was being carried to Belthane the strain put on the rope by his weight had tightened the knots that were in it, and this had created a small amount of slack. By bending his knees as much as possible without drawing Belthane's attention from her dancing, Longarm had kept busy flexing his thigh and calf muscles against his bonds.

He'd felt only a small amount of slack in the rope at first, but now it had increased—not greatly, but enough to give him hope that when he could work unobserved he'd be able to stretch his bonds still further. He kept moving his legs, tightening the long muscles in their calves and pushing first one foot and then the other against the rope that held them, and at the same time exerting all the effort he could muster to help them by adding to his pushing the force of the bigger and more powerful muscles in his thighs.

Longarm's efforts had yielded only small results when Belthane suddenly ended her dance with a wild shout that seemed to be pulled from the depths of her throat. Her exertions had brought a flush to her face and had brought out the buds of her full breasts. Their tips pushed forward now like small, blunt fingers.

At any other time, perhaps with another woman, Longarm might have taken pleasure in what he saw. Belthane's exposed body did not stir him. He turned his eyes to the ceiling of the cavern and stared at it.

"Don't act as if you scorn me, human!" Belthane said. "Too many men have praised the beauty of my form for your pretenses to deceive me!"

When Longarm made no effort to reply she moved closer to him and stepped with one foot across his hips to stand above him, looking down at him. Longarm met

126

her eyes without flinching and without letting any feeling show in his. Belthane bent forward, then hunkered down, her feet still planted on the outsides of his thighs.

"I'll soon find out what my servants have brought me," she said.

Her hands worked at Longarm's belt buckle, then moved down to the buttons of his trousers' fly. With the quick facility that spoke of past experience, she undid the buttons and yanked the placket open. Her nostrils dilated angrily and her brows drew together in a frown when she saw Longarm's long johns, but she worked at the bottom buttons of its placket until she'd freed them as well. Then she jerked the seams apart and stared at his crotch.

"What kind of man are you?" she demanded when she saw that Longarm had remained flaccid. "A poor one, not a full man, one who can't rise to fill a woman's needs?"

Knowing what he was risking, but deciding after a split second of thought that the risk was worthwhile if it threw Belthane off balance and gave him a chance to break free, Longarm said, "A real woman. Maybe not one that calls herself a witch."

"I *am* a witch!" Belthane insisted, her voice sharp with anger. "But what are you and who are you? There is not a mortal man on earth who can resist our Craft!" Then before an instant had passed she caught herself, and smiled. It was a smile of triumph blended with evil. She went on, "There is no man alive who can scorn Belthane! And I will prove it to you now!"

Concentrating now, Belthane turned her full attention to Longarm. She stroked and squeezed and caressed him, first with her fingers, then with the tips of her breasts. When these attentions did not bring Longarm to

127

respond, she kneeled across his thighs and cradled him in the cleft of her full breasts, squeezing her globes together to hold him pressed close, bathed in warmth and smooth softness, while she writhed her body trying to excite him. He still managed to stay flaccid even when she straddled his thighs with her knees and held herself poised above him and pressed his lax shaft into the vee of her thighs while writhing and bathing him in the warmth of her nether lips.

With his hands still cuffed behind him and his ankles bound tightly, Longarm was unable to avoid her caresses or to resist them, but by concentrating all his efforts on his own stratagem, he managed to continue keeping himself from responding. Finding a way to escape was still uppermost in his mind, and he shut off the stirring that Belthane was arousing in him in order to meet his own goal.

At last Belthane stopped her fruitless efforts. She raised herself on her heels, her knees still astraddle Longarm's hips, and looked down at him. Her naked body gleamed with perspiration, her hair was in greater disarray than ever, and her face was twisted into an expression that revealed both her anger and her disappointment.

"You are indeed a stubborn man!" she said. Her voice was gasping as she panted for breath between words, but her tone was still sharp and angry. She went on, "But no one bests Belthane! I'd meant to save my finest caresses until later, but now I must use them! I will not let a mere mortal man defeat me!"

Now Belthane moved with slow deliberateness. She bent forward and cradled Longarm's flaccid cylinder between her palms. For a moment she rubbed her hands along it, then she bent forward and engulfed him with her swollen lips.

Longarm had been expecting a move such as this. He kept his eyes off Belthane and stared up at the cavern's dark ceiling, where the light of the candle faded into obscurity and hid the roof of the cavern in darkness. His long resistance to Belthane's continually insistent caresses had been interrupted by their brief exchange. Longarm found that he could still prevent himself from beginning an erection, but Belthane's long period of trying had weakened his control. At last his body overcame his will and he jetted.

Belthane lifted her head and released Longarm at once when his quick spasm ended, but she did not leave him, as he'd expected her to do. Instead she shifted her body and straddled his hips, and before he realized her intention she'd lowered herself onto him. Then she began a steady rhythmic rocking while a weird chant in a language that was strange to Longarm poured from her puffed lips.

Engulfed in a greater warmth than before, Longarm found to his surprise that he could no longer hold back nature's forces. He felt himself swelling and becoming rigid, and Belthane also felt the change that was occurring. She continued her chant as she crouched above him, her eyes gleaming down on him, as she began wriggling her hips once more.

Longarm fought to regain his control, but from the start it was a losing battle. Hampered by his bonds, he could do nothing but lie still while Belthane writhed and bucked above him. Even though he made no effort to prolong their embrace, it seemed to him that a long time went by before Belthane cried out triumphantly when he peaked and began to jet.

She prolonged their embrace until Longarm once again grew limp, and when she did bring herself to her knees again and looked down on him, her body glistened with the sweat that her exertions had brought— but there was a gleam of triumph in her eyes.

"You could not hope to win against my powers over the dark spirits," she gloated. "Now you belong to me until I choose to release you or kill you!"

Longarm knew that he could not appear to be touched by her threat. He said calmly, "Maybe it's the other way around, Belthane. You might be a witch, like you say you are, but don't forget you're a woman, too. And a woman bonds to a man a lot easier than he does to her."

Belthane's face contorted angrily and her mouth opened as though she were going to lash out at him, then she smiled. In spite of her regular features and statuesque figure, evil showed in her eyes as she exclaimed, "No! You are only an ordinary man. I have never seen one yet who can hold himself against my powers. You are mine, to use you as I wish to. But you'll find me a kind mistress—until I tire of you."

Longarm caught a hint of fatigue in Belthane's voice and did not answer her. She stood looking at him, still naked, then her body sagged perceptibly. She bent to pick up her robe, and as she stood up, said, "I will sleep now. Later, I will come to you again, and when I do you will no longer be able to resist my spells. Then I will place you in my cone of power and teach you what it means to be bonded to a witch!"

Without looking back at him, Belthane walked away. Only a few steps took her into the darkness beyond the glow cast by the candle, and Longarm lost sight of her.

For several minutes he lay without moving, thinking

that Belthane might be watching him from the darkness beyond the feeble circle of light cast by the candle. He listened carefully for any noise that might betray her presence, but the cavern was totally silent. Not even the whispering pattering feet of a mouse scurrying around broke the stillness.

When he was sure that he was alone and unwatched, Longarm began to carry out the plan he'd had to form so quickly. Rolling onto his side, he bent his knees to bring his feet up behind his back. His bound wrists hampered the motion of his hands, and the rope that secured his ankles kept him from bending one knee at a time, which would have allowed him to stretch and bend his legs freely.

He was unable to see either his hands or his feet in spite of the candle's light. Each time he turned his head to peer over his shoulder in order to guide his efforts he found that no matter what position he might twist himself into, he could not make them come together. In spite of the soreness that soon took over his muscles, already bruised by the hard handling given him by Percy Moore's helpers, Longarm persisted. Finally, after more than a dozen tries, he felt his fingertips brush against the leather of his boot uppers.

After that, it was a matter of time and patience. He moved slowly and carefully as he inched his hand down to get a firm grip on the top of his bootleg, then pulled his feet up to the point where his fingers could be slipped into the boot's uppers to fish out his handcuff key. Holding it tightly, not risking dropping it on the floor, he began maneuvering his hands, bending his wrists in the tightest arc he could manage, until his efforts came to an end when he slid the key into the lock of one of his handcuffs.

Three minutes later Longarm was free once more, but though he'd gotten rid of his bonds he was not yet ready to leap into action. His hands were still so numb that his fingers almost failed him when he buttoned the fly of his trousers and buckled his belt. He began opening and closing his hands to restore the flexibility of his fingers.

His legs needed more attention than his hands. They had been bound so tightly for so many hours that his feet had almost no feeling, and with each step he took his knees threatened to collapse under his weight. Longarm began walking back and forth in the small circle of candlelight while he opened and closed his hands, and as his blood began to circulate with freedom the limberness gradually returned to his fingers and his legs.

When he was sure that he could trust his fingers not to fumble anything they tried to hold, he picked up his handcuffs and hung them on his belt, then fished his derringer out of his vest pocket. As he tucked the deadly little weapon behind his belt buckle, Longarm wondered how Percival Moore and his crew could have overlooked it when they tied him up.

That thought set him to speculating about time. He had no idea how long it had been since he drank the drugged cider, how long he'd been unconscious, how much time he'd spent in the hands of Belthane, and whether it was daylight or darkness outside the cavern. He was suddenly aware that he was ravenously hungry, and from the growling of his stomach he decided that quite some time, perhaps as long as a night, possibly even a night and part or all of a day, had passed since his last meal.

"Not that it makes much difference, old son," Longarm told himself in a half whisper. "The thing you better be worrying about is finding that woman and tying her up, then figuring out where there's a place to get outa this cave, and then how long it's going to take you to get to that blamed constable's house when you do get out. So just start eating the apple one bite at a time."

Longarm started toward the darkness beyond the circle of candlelight, heading for the spot where he'd last seen Belthane before she disappeared. He moved as softly as he could, taking careful steps ahead, planting his forward foot softly and testing the surface on which his boot sole rested before bringing up his other foot to complete his step.

In spite of his caution, as his weight fell on his freshly placed boot sole, there was a tiny scraping noise from the stone floor that sounded very loud indeed in the utter silence. He reached the tall candelabrum, and the musky penetrating scent which he'd been aware of since regaining his senses was almost overwhelmingly strong. He hurried past the candle and stopped at the point where its light merged with the darkness. Somewhere in the blackness ahead he could hear the soft susurrus of someone breathing.

Almost certain now that except for himself the only person in that part of the vast cavern must be Belthane, Longarm continued his cautious advance. Because he was moving so slowly, the adjustment of his eyes from the area lighted dimly by the candle to the almost complete darkness beyond reach of its flickering rays was almost as automatic as nature had intended.

A vague form loomed in front of him, outlined against a lighter area still farther ahead, and when he advanced another careful half step Longarm saw that he'd encountered a chair. Then he grew aware of a soft vague rhythmic sound in the still-impenetrable blackness. He moved carefully up to the chair and stopped beside it. Grudgingly, bit by bit, his eyes grew accustomed to the darker area in front of him.

A puddled blotch of lesser shadow took shape as he peered at the area beyond the chair. Then Longarm realized that the light rhythmic noise of which he'd gradually become aware was someone breathing, and simple logic told him that the person who was breathing must be Belthane. He froze where he stood and peered through the gloom. Bit by bit, as though he were watching the composition of a mosaic, the bed and the woman sleeping on it became individual, definable forms.

Belthane's sprawled body was a shadow upon the lighter rectangle of the bed. Its outline against the bedclothes was not really visible, but the darker blobs formed by her hair, the rosettes of her breasts, and the triangular pubic brush enabled Longarm to judge the location of her arms and legs and allowed him to plan his next moves. As he stood studying the big rectangle of her bed, Longarm now became aware of the light susurrus of her breathing. It was regular and even, an indication that she was sleeping soundly.

Nevertheless, he did not relax his concentration as he left his observation spot and moved with infinite caution up to the edge of the bed. He stopped there, looking down at the sleeping woman. Belthane lay in a sprawl, one arm outstretched, the other lying aslant across her torso. One of her legs was stretched out straight, while the other was crooked into a triangle with her knee at its tip. He was close enough now when he studied her face to make out the short dark lines of her brows, the lashes that fringed her closed eyes, and the lighter hue of her lips.

Moving with the same slow care that had made his

approach successful, Longarm fished out his bandanna and tucked it loosely into the cuff of a shirtsleeve. Then he slid his handcuffs from his belt and muffled with his palm the slight metallic rasping made when he opened them. Holding the manacles in one hand, he brought to completion the plan that he'd been forming since his first glimpse of the sleeping woman.

Bending above Belthane, Longarm crammed the bandanna into her half-open mouth. While she was still half-asleep, he pulled her wrists together and clamped the handcuffs around them. Belthane was still trying to push the bandanna from her mouth with her tongue when Longarm closed his hand over her jaws, clamping her lips closed.

Belatedly, Belthane had now begun to struggle. Her torso arched as she tried to pull her wrists free from the manacles and her head swiveled in spite of Longarm's grip over her mouth. At the same time her feet were flailing, the wild kicks thudding almost inaudibly against the mattress.

"It's not going to do you a bit of good to fight this way," Longarm told her. He did not raise his voice above a conversational level. "And from all I heard about witches back in West Virginia where I grew up, there ain't no witches' charms that work against iron and steel. So you might as well settle down. Then as soon as you feel like talking, you and me will have a nice little gabfest, and if you got any sense left after this show you been putting on, you'll tell me exactly what this witching skulduggery is all about."

# Chapter 11

With the gag in her mouth, Belthane was unable to
reply to Longarm, but her dark eyes did all the talking
that was necessary. The deep gloom that shrouded the
bed did not hide the anger that twisted her face into a
scowl as she continued to stare at him while the realization that she was indeed helpless was sinking home.

"I'll just get that oversized candlestick you got sitting
in the other room. Then we'll be able to see each other
while we have our little talk," Longarm told her.

He took the few steps needed to reach the candelabrum and brought it back. Trying to ignore the musky
scent that it diffused as its flame flickered, he placed it
between the chair and bed. In its new position the big
candle shed enough light to give Longarm a clear view
of Belthane and the adjoining area from which he'd just
escaped. Returning to the place where he'd freed himself from his bonds, he picked up the length of rope that
had held his ankles and used it to bind Belthane's feet
together. Then he sat down and took out a cigar.

"I'm not forgetting that you can't talk till I get that
gag outa your mouth," he went on, holding a match
ready to strike. "But till I got some idea about what I'm
up against here, I aim to pop you a few questions that
you can answer just by nodding yes or shaking your
head no. And it won't do you a bit of good to lay there
and be stubborn. I got all the time in the world to spend
getting the answers I'm after."

Belthane had kept her gaze on Longarm while he
talked, but when he'd dragged his thumbnail over the

match and lit his cigar, then returned his attention to her, Belthane had closed her eyes. He said nothing, but settled back in the chair and puffed his long slim cigar as though he had no thought for anything except enjoying it.

Moment followed moment while the stillness between them seemed to deepen. Longarm kept no track of the time, but he knew the only way he had of persuading Belthane to give him the information he was after was by showing greater patience than she did. He'd smoked half his cigar in long-spaced puffs before she opened her eyes and looked at him. After she'd studied his set face for several moments she nodded and started twisting her head.

"I guess you finally got something to say to me?" he asked. Longarm's voice was level and noncommital, almost casual. When Belthane nodded, he went on, hoping as he spoke that she would not see through his bluff. "Before I take off that gag so's you can talk, maybe I better tell you something else. I've had some time to puzzle over this mess you and your men have made here in Salem. I got a pretty good idea what's been going on, so there ain't no use in you trying to string out a bunch of lies. You figure you can stick to the truth?"

Belthane nodded vigorously.

Longarm went on, "Now there's one more thing. If I take that gag outa your mouth and you start yelling for them fellows that toted me here, I'll stuff it back in quicker'n you can say Jack Robinson, and you'll swing on the gallows with the rest of 'em. You understand that?"

Again Belthane nodded. Longarm stood up and went to the bed where he removed the bandanna from her mouth.

Belthane began talking almost before Longarm had finished removing the gag. "Because I choose to talk does not mean you have defeated me," she said, spitting out the words in an angry stream. Then her face underwent a lightninglike change. The scowl vanished and her voice dropped to a persuasive whisper as she went on, "You must be spawn of Lucifer, as I am, to have overcome me as you did! Let us join—"

Longarm's hand darted out and closed over her mouth. With her wrists and ankles pinioned, Belthane could do nothing except writhe like a huge serpent, even when Longarm pressed her head down onto the bed. She kicked and wriggled and tried to break free, but even when she tried to close her teeth in the flesh of his palm he kept her lips sealed.

"Maybe you weren't listening to what I said a minute ago," he said, making his voice as harsh and menacing as he knew how. With his free hand he picked up the bandanna and flicked it in front of her eyes. "I don't tell nobody what I aim to do unless I'm ready to do it. Now make up your mind fast, before I stuff this in your mouth again. If I got to do that, I'll just go find out what I need to know without asking you any more questions."

Abruptly, Belthane let all her muscles relax and lay supine on the bed again. She lay motionless for a few moments, then Longarm felt her try to move her head in a nod of agreement. He took his hand off her mouth.

"Go on," he commanded harshly. "Start talking."

Her face still sullen as she gasped for breath between words, she said, "If you go along the passage on the right side it will take you to the small cellar the constable calls his jail. If you go in the other direction it will take you to his home."

"Have I got to go through any doors to get to where he lives?"

Belthane shook her head. "No."

"Are there any side passages I might get into by mistake?"

She repeated her head shake without speaking.

"Does anybody but you stay down here all the time?"

Again Belthane shook her head.

Longarm was silent for a moment. He knew the ticklish part of his questioning still lay ahead, and decided to lay a false trail, one that might lure Belthane into answering the key questions that loomed so large in his mind. He asked, "How's your daddy take to you getting mixed up in all this witchery stuff?"

Belthane stared at him as though she had not understood his question, and said nothing.

"You ain't going to be able to fool me," Longarm went on quietly. "I might not've tumbled to who you are if it hadn't been for me seeing Ellie and the doctor before I ran into you. He's your daddy, isn't he? And Ellie's your sister, or I miss my guess."

"Ellie is a fool!" she blurted.

Longarm realized that his question had done two things: It had caught Belthane off guard, and at the same time touched a very sensitive nerve. Obeying the lawman's instinct that had been his guide for so many years, he pressed on, "You two're twins, I bet. How come you're so different in everything but looks?"

"She is a fool!" Belthane repeated. "Together there is no force in the world that could overcome us! Apart, our power is cut in half!"

"Then Ellie don't hold with what you're doing?"

"She would be here, if she did! And with us using our powers together we would have beaten you!"

139

"How about your daddy? The doctor?"

"He was the first to recognize my gift," Belthane boasted. "He is from Old Salem, where our family settled long ago."

Longarm was beginning to see a pattern emerging now. He also saw that Ellie was a bad subject for discussing with Belthane and began changing the line of his questioning.

"I guess there's others here that come from your old home?"

"Enough to matter. Here we are creating a new realm, one that will be ruled by our mystic powers."

"You feel like telling me about them powers?"

Belthane shook her head. "It is forbidden. Only adepts in the Craft are allowed to know."

"How about them three fellows the constable had with him when they lugged me in here," Longarm went on, "I guess they're the kind you're talking about?"

"Of course. They know as much of the Craft as they are allowed."

"How many more has he got in his gang?"

"It is not his gang!" Belthane protested. "They are my acolytes! I let him lead them only when it suits my purpose!"

"You didn't answer my question," he pointed out.

"I have more than three acolytes!" she replied, her voice boastful now. "Many more than even you can overcome! And when I am free—"

"Don't count too much on getting free," Longarm broke in. "I sure ain't aiming to turn you loose."

"You will have no choice!"

"As long as I stay on my pins and keep my hands loose and keep you right there where you are, it's you that ain't got a choice," Longarm said quickly. "Now, I got another question or two that I wanta ask you—"

"Asking them will be useless," Belthane interrupted him to say. "I will tell you nothing more."

For a moment Longarm debated the choices he had. He could let the questions that were still in his mind wait for a more promising time, or press on while Belthane was still helpless. He now had a working knowledge of the problem he faced, and decided that speed of action was more important than further knowledge, which, given the change in Belthane's mood, might or might not be forthcoming.

"Well, you've told me just about everything I was after," he said. "Now I got to get busy."

"Busy with what?"

"Straightening out a few of the things that's wrong around here. And seeing as I have to leave you by yourself, I guess I better make sure you don't get off to someplace where I'd have to chase you down and bring you back."

"There is no power you can use to hold me where I do not wish to be!" Belthane boasted.

Longarm was not impressed. He said dryly, "Maybe not. But even if that rope and them handcuffs have done a pretty good job so far, I don't aim to take any chances."

When she made no reply, Longarm picked up the long black dress which Belthane had discarded. He had no rope, but this was not the first time he'd had to improvise in tying up a prisoner. Taking out his pocketknife, he began sawing at the wide bottom hem of the robe. Belthane watched, her scowling face showing her anger, as he cut the hem off the garment.

When the hem was freed Longarm held a strip of doubled cloth that was almost a dozen feet long. He looped one end around the thick wooden stretcher that ran the length of the bed and knotted it tightly. Then he tossed the long loose end across Belthane's shoulders to the opposite side. He looped the center of the strip around Belthane's neck, then, guaging its tension carefully, he pulled the free end around the stretcher on the opposite side of the bed and knotted it in place.

"You'll be all right as long as you lay still," he told Belthane as he tested the tension of the fabric strip. "This ain't going to choke you as long as you don't move or try to get up. But the minute you start moving around, you'll be in real trouble." While he was warning her, Longarm picked up the gag that he'd used earlier. He went on, "I don't figure there's anybody close enough to this place to hear you, but just to be safe—"

Belthane had been watching Longarm as she listened to his carefully casual monologue. When he broke off suddenly and wrapped the gag around her mouth in a single quick move, she began to struggle. The loop of fabric circling her neck tightened as she tried to raise her head and escape being gagged, but when she found herself struggling for breath she fell back quickly. She lay motionless while Longarm finished his job of securing her.

Standing beside the bed, he said, "You'll be all right as long as you lay still. I'm not going very far, just to sorta look around and find out how the land lays. There ain't much chance of you getting free, but even if you do, I'll catch up with you in no time."

Even before he began questioning Belthane, Longarm had realized that he must scout around the cavern, not only to find a way out, but to be sure that it held no hidden surprises that might cause trouble for him later. He took out his knife and stepped up to the candelabrum, ignoring the perfume it was diffusing, and began sawing at the candle midway between the base of its stand and the burning wick.

Belthane watched him with angry eyes while he cut the candle into halves and lighted the section remaining in the holder from the flickering wick of the half that he now held. With the light in the cavern doubled, Longarm could see for several yards along both of the passages that led from the wide chamber they were in. He'd lost all sense of direction during the time when he'd been unconscious, but unless Belthane had been lying to him, he was reasonably sure that he was in the branch of the passage that led to the storm cellar.

"I got good ears," he warned Belthane as he turned away from his examination of the tunnels. "So you just better lay quiet and not try to get away while I'm seeing what this place is like. I don't imagine I'll have very far to go to find out what I need to know, and I'll be keeping an ear cocked in this direction while I look around."

Holding his half candle high, Longarm started along the stone floor of the tunnel to his right. He counted his steps as he made his way along the passage. After his counting had reached twenty paces the passageway narrowed, but there was still room for two, perhaps even for three men to walk abreast.

Another half dozen paces brought him to a halt, facing an arched wooden door. The door was hung between bricked pillars, and Longarm frowned as he looked at them, for the bricks appeared to him to be identical with those that he'd seen lining Moore's storm cellar. He pressed an ear to the rough cool boards, but heard nothing. He pushed the boards, gently and experimentally at first, then with more force, but even when he put his shoulder to them the door did not budge.

When he held his candle closer to the stone pillar at one side of the door he saw nothing except the thin crack where the door and pillar came together. Then he turned his attention to the opposite edge, and found a small recess chiseled into the stone. He poked his fingers into the little opening and they encountered the cold metal tongue of a latch. He lifted the latch and the door swung open.

Even before he entered the chamber beyond, Longarm was sure of what he'd find, and as he stepped through the portal the candle's light revealed nothing surprising. He was in the storm cellar that Moore had showed him.

A glance was all Longarm needed to see that nothing had been changed since the constable showed him the cellar on the day before. He turned to examine the interior side of the door he'd just opened, and found a small masterpiece of concealment had been created by whoever built the circular cellar. The interior side of the door had been carefully and skillfully faced with boards cut and planed to look like bricks and curved to join perfectly the contours of the cellar's wall. The boards had been grooved and painted to match the wall so closely that when Longarm had studied the latch for a moment and closed the door he could scarcely tell where it was located.

"Well, old son, it looks like you got a way out now," Longarm told himself, his voice a half whisper. "And it's a pretty safe bet that when you try going down the other end of this tunnel, you'll wind up in that constable's home."

Stepping across to the outer door, he spent several minutes working at the latch, and at last succeeded in tripping it. When a rim of daylight showed in the cracks around the door's edges he slitted his eyes and opened it a bit wider. The fading reddish sunlight that trickled through the narrow opening was still bright enough to start him blinking, but the red hue of the light signaled that sunset was drawing close, and there were things that he needed to do before darkness fell. He closed the door quickly and crossed the room to the hidden door that led into the underground passage.

Both satisfied and displeased with what he'd discovered, Longarm started back down the underground passage. When he reached the chamber where he'd left Belthane he found her still lying passively on the bed. Her eyes were closed when he got his first glimpse of her, but suddenly she opened them and turned her head to look at him. From the look in her eyes, Longarm saw that she wanted to talk to him again. He stepped up to the bed and removed the gag.

"When are you going to come to your senses and release me?" she asked as soon as her lips were free. "My coven will return soon, then all the time you have spent will amount to nothing."

"I reckon that's a chance I have to take," Longarm told her. "But if Percy Moore and them other fellows that lugged me down here is what you call your coven, I wouldn't want to bet on them. I heard you tell them not to come back till you went and called them, which you ain't about to do, tied up here."

"Bonds are made to be broken!" she said angrily.

"Breaking 'em's easier said than done. Anyway, I'm going looking for your bunch myself, right this minute."

"You cannot harm them while they are under the shield of my protection!"

"Well, now," Longarm replied, "it's just fine with me if you and them believe that, but I don't happen to. So

145

you'll have to put up with staying where you are, and I'll go take care of the business I still got to finish."

Stepping up to the candelabrum, Longarm extinguished the flickering wick. Carrying the piece of candle he'd used before, he started along the tunnel that led to Percy Moore's house. It was much longer than the one which led to the storm cellar, but it ended at the same sort of door that he'd encountered there, and tripping the lock open was no problem.

He pushed the door open a crack and listened, but heard no voices or sounds of motion in the house. Opening the door wider, Longarm stepped through it and found himself in the constable's kitchen.

There was a coffeepot and stewpan on the cast-iron range, but both were cold to his touch. The unpainted table under the window was strewn with dirty dishes and used cups, but there was one familiar object in the clutter that drew his eyes like a magnet. Stepping to the table, Longarm picked up his Colt, its butt settling into his palm like the handshake of an old friend.

A quick glance at the side of the cylinder showed the glint of brass shell-bases, but Longarm took no chances. He pulled the hammer to half cock and rotated the cylinder, removing and examining each cartridge in turn to be sure none of them had been tampered with. As far as he could tell, the cartridges were those he'd slid into the cylinder himself. Satisfied at last, he holstered the Colt and restored his derringer to its customary place in his vest pocket.

"Now, old son, you can get along with the rest of the job you got to do," he told himself.

Leaving the house, Longarm started walking toward the stable through the fast-fading light, hoping his horse would be there. It was, and his saddle was resting on the hay-strewn ground just inside the door. He made a quick job of saddling the livery mount and headed for Salem's main and only street.

Darkness was settling in by the time Longarm reached the first of the town's widely spaced houses, and in the few dwellings he passed on his way there lights were already showing in the windows. The doctor's house was dark and from a distance looked deserted, but just as Longarm reined in a light appeared in one of the windows, a thin line of brightness only a fraction of an inch thick outlining the narrow space between the window's frame and its inside shade.

Draping his horse's reins through the iron loop of the hitching post in front of the house, Longarm went up the steps and tapped at the door. In a moment light footsteps sounded on the other side of the door, a key grated in the lock, and the door opened. Ellie stood in the doorway, outlined in the dim glow of lamplight that spilled from a room down the hall.

"Marshal Long!" she exclaimed. "I'm ever so glad to see you—" she stopped short, a worried frown creeping over her face as she went on, "I guess I am, anyhow."

"If you don't mind me saying so, Miss Ellie, you sound like you're sorta mixed up," Longarm said.

"I—I guess I am," she said absently. "But when Father left he warned me not to open the door for anybody who knocked, and I guess he meant you just as well as everybody else."

"Your daddy's not home, then?"

Ellie shook her head. "No. He went out with Uncle Clete about, well, it was quite a long time ago, I don't remember exactly when."

Longarm was becoming aware of some change that had taken place in Ellie's manner since his last visit, and

147

he remembered at once where he'd last heard the name Clete.

"Now, I don't imagine your daddy intended for you to shut out somebody like me," he told Ellie. "I'm sworn to uphold the law, and I sure don't mean no harm to you. If you don't mind me stepping inside, Ellie, I think you and me better have a little talk."

"I, I guess it'll be all right," she said. There was still hesitancy in her voice and manner, but she stepped out of the doorway to let Longarm enter. "And I don't know what it is that's bothering me so, but I've got the strangest feeling about Father. I feel like I ought to be with him, that he's in some kind of trouble."

# Chapter 12

"What kinda trouble, Ellie?" Longarm asked as she closed and locked the door behind him. When she turned back to face him with the light behind her he was struck by her resemblance to Belthane.

"I don't know, and that's what bothers me," she said.

"Your daddy goes out to see sick people all the time, I'd imagine," Longarm pointed out. "Do you fret like this every time he's a little bit late getting back?"

"No, of course not. But, well, Uncle Clete acted like he was upset. Father took him into his consulting room, and they were in there for a long time. Then Father said he had to go out and he seemed sort of worried, the same way Uncle Clete was."

"This Uncle Clete you've mentioned, is he your uncle on your daddy's side, or your mama's?" Longarm asked as he followed Ellie down the hall toward the patch of light that spilled from the open door of the parlor. They went in and Ellie motioned to a chair.

"Neither one, Marshal," she replied as Longarm sat down and she settled onto the divan. "He isn't a real kinfolk kind of uncle. I just started calling him that when I was a little girl, and, well, I still do."

"I see," he said with a nod. "His folks moved here when your family did, then?"

"Of course. Most of the families here were in the same covered-wagon train that came here from Old Salem. But that was a long time ago."

"And there's some of the real old-timers left, I guess?"

Ellied nodded her head. "Yes. I think the oldest one is Uncle Perc. He's the constable now."

"Constable Moore?"

"Of course. I know you've met him, Marshal."

"I sure have. And I think I better go see if I can find him right now, Ellie." Longarm stood up. "You'll be all right here until your pa gets back, just keep the doors locked, like you've been doing."

"Is something wrong, Marshal Long?" Ellie asked as she followed Longarm down the hall to the door. "Even if there is, I don't suppose Father would've told me. He treats me like I'm still just a little girl."

"I guess there's always something wrong in every town in the world, Ellie," Longarm repplied as he unlocked the door and opened it. "But right now I got to take care of this case I'm on. You just sit tight here and keep the door locked, like you've been doing. The doctor'll be getting back pretty soon."

Longarm kept the livery horse at a brisk clip as he rode through the darkness back to Constable Moore's house. The house was unlighted, and while he was reasonably sure no one would be on lookout inside, he took no chances. Angling away from the house, he rode in a half circle around it and approached it from the side where the barn would hide him. He left the horse standing in the darkness and moved on foot for the short distance that remained.

Coming up to the back of the dwelling, he tried the kitchen door and found it unlocked. Stepping inside, he stood listening for a moment in the inside gloom, and when he could make out the vague forms of the kitchen stove and table, he used them to orient himself as he made his way to the wall in which the hidden door leading to the cavern had been concealed. The door was not latched, and when he pulled it open the gloom beyond put the night's blackness to shame.

Longarm reached into his vest pocket for a match, and his fingertips told him that he was running low. Leaving the cave's door ajar, he stepped to the kitchen stove. As he'd thought he would, he found a box of sulfur matches on the shelf above the cooking surface, and helped himself to a generous handful.

Tucking the matches into his vest pocket as he moved he went back to the door, where the yawning entrance to the underground witches' retreat stood out like an inkblot on gray paper. Longarm stepped inside and descended the short flight of stairs until his boot soles grated on the stone floor of the underground cavern. Keeping his left hand within reach of the stone wall, and reaching out to touch it now and then as he moved, he started ahead through the impenetrable blackness.

With his sense of touch the only guide he could rely on, Longarm was forced to walk at a slower pace than he'd have chosen if he could have depended on his eyes. It seemed to him that he was progressing at a snail's slow pace, and when a dim shimmer of light appeared ahead and grew steadily brighter, he sped up.

From the moment he'd seen the glow in front of him he'd been sure that the light came from what he'd come to think of as Belthane's bedchamber. He was not at all surprised when he rounded a jog in the tunnel's walls and entered a stretch that was brightly lighted in comparison with the area he'd just left. His guess that the light marked Belthane's bedchamber was correct. The bed in which he'd left her tied and helpless was tousled and empty, but the short stub that had been in the candelabrum at that time had now been replaced with a fresh tall candle.

Longarm had expected that Belthane would have been freed by now. He did not stop to examine the bedchamber, but plunged ahead. He was on familiar ground now, no longer worried about what lay ahead. As he'd remembered, the cavern ran in a fairly straight line, and he made good progress. He'd reached a point where the light from behind began to be overcome again by darkness when he saw a dark bundle on the corridor floor.

Longarm stopped at once. The bundle had not been there when he'd passed this spot earlier. He stood in the shadows while he studied the dark shapeless bulk on the floor. It was a large bundle, and for a fleeting moment Longarm took the bundle to be a man stretched prone. He stopped, his hand darting to his Colt, his eyes fixed on the object ahead. He kept the revolver in his hand as he edged forward, but the shadowed heap stayed motionless. He'd gotten almost close enough to touch the dark, oddly shaped blob before he could be sure that what he was looking at was indeed a man stretched prone—a very dead man.

A thick quilt was spread over the corpse from the waist up, and its sprawling legs were twisted into angles that no living man could achieve or endure. Longarm bent to pull the concealing fabric aside. The body lay facedown, arms upraised, twisted legs splayed wide. Longarm was forced to drop to one knee in order to handle the bulky cover as he pulled it aside and struck a match in order to get a clear look at the corpse. In spite of the distortion and the uncertain light, Longarm recognized the dead man. He was Dr. Parent.

Longarm was looking at the head of the dead man in profile, but even by the flickering uncertain light of the dying match he could tell that his face was grotesquely distorted, puffed and strangely elongated. There was no question about the cause of the doctor's death. A black-rimmed hole was in his forehead and trickles of dry blood ran down his cheeks.

Longarm had seen such distorted faces before, on the bodies of men who'd been shot with a large-caliber pistol pushed against their heads and held firmly to muffle the noise of the shot. Not only did the bullet tear through their skull and brains, the lead slug was followed by the gasses created by the powder's ignition. Expanding explosively, these gasses would crack the victim's cheekbones and jawbones and stretch his head to distort his facial features.

"You got a puzzle on your hands now, old son," he told himself. Though he spoke in his normal conversational tone, his voice seemed loud in the silence. "From everything that girl Belthane said, her daddy was one of the head men of them witches, so they must've had some kind of falling out, and Moore and his bunch decided to get rid of him. And you got an ugly job to take care of, too. Looks like it's going to be up to you to tell that nice little Ellie that her daddy's been murdered."

Longarm lifted his hand to pull a cheroot from his pocket and realized that he was still holding the quilt which had been spread over the doctor's body. He flicked it aside, then as the thick quilt unfolded and dropped, his sharp eyes caught sight of several charred spots with holes torn in their centers. He toed the quilt to spread it flat on the stone floor.

When the quilt lay flat a half dozen charred, bullet-torn and bloodstained patches were revealed. The stains and torn spots told Longarm that the doctor's murder was not the first in which the quilt had played a part.

153

The pattern of the torn, blotched, and bloodstained areas showed that a gun wrapped in the thick quilt had been pressed firmly against the victim before it was fired. Counting the torn areas was impossible, for in places they merged and overlapped, but it was plain to him that the quilt had been used as a gun-blast muzzler several times.

Though Longarm had seen few such examples before, he'd learned from those earlier cases that when a gun muffled in such a manner was fired the report of its discharge was a noise no louder than a sneeze. With the weapon swathed as it was, the gasses created by the ignited gunpowder were unable to spurt and spread by following the bullet from the muzzle, nor could they escape through the small gap between the cylinder's revolving chamber and its barrel. As a consequence, most of their expansive force followed the path of the bullet, and distorted the victim's head and face. The noise of the shot would not have been heard by someone only a few feet away.

"It ain't no wonder that nobody had ever heard any shooting when one of them dead bodies showed up," he said under his breath. "Whoever's been triggering off that quiet gun had to know exactly what they were doing."

Folding the tattered, bloodstained quilt carefully to preserve the evidence it contained, Longarm looked around for a place to hide it. The bare walls and stone floor of the corridor offered no opportunity to hide a toothpick, and there was not even a dark corner where with luck it might be overlooked. To preserve the evidence he'd uncovered, Longarm hurried back to Belthane's bed and tucked the folded quilt under it where he was sure the darkness would keep it from being noticed.

Then he hurried back to the body, but this time he did not stop. He went on to the hidden door of the storm cellar.

When he pressed his ear against the door, he could hear nothing—no voices, no sounds of movement—that would tell him whether the room was empty or occupied. Longarm decided quickly that if he took a chance of opening the door, the result would be worth the risk. He slid his fingers into the recess that hid the lock mechanism and tripped the latch. The door swung open a crack, and lamplight flooded through the finger-thin slit. With the light came the sound of voices.

". . . as long as that damn federal marshal's on the loose," a man was saying. Longarm recognized the voice. The speaker was Constable Moore.

"Now, just don't look at me such a funny way when you say that, Perc," another man protested. His voice, too, was familiar. Longarm recognized it at once, although as yet he could not match a name to it. The speaker was one of the men who'd carried him from Moore's house to the cavern where Belthane lived.

"Like I told you," the man when on, "Belthane didn't want us around while she was working on him."

Now Belthane spoke for the first time. "Yes, part of the blame is mine," she agreed. "I did not take the time needed to draw a pentagram, or the man would not have escaped."

"That federal marshal is just one of the things we've got to take care of fast," a second man broke in. Again, Longarm recognized the voice as that of another of his recent captors. "We no longer have Swein. Where will we find another doctor who's of the Old Religion? We need one to sign death certificates and do all the other things Swein did to keep outsiders from learning that we practice the Ancient Crafts."

A frown had formed on Longarm's face when the name Swein was first mentioned, but now he understood that it was the secret name used by the doctor when he was working with the witches' coven.

"Now, that clears up a lot of things that you been puzzling about, old son," he muttered. Then Moore started speaking again and he returned his full attention to the conversation in the cellar.

"We'll find another doctor easily enough," the constable assured his companions. "There are covens of us in Fort Worth and San Antonio and Galveston. All we will need to do is to spread the word that we need a doctor, and one will be glad to join us here."

Longarm's frown returned when he heard the names of the largest cities in Texas mentioned. Then Belthane began talking again, and he gave his full attention to listening to her.

"It's as well Swein has gone to join the other restless spirits. Now I can bring Ellie into our coven. I've asked her before to join us, and she's always refused. Each time I've asked her she's said that Swein needed her."

"And what did Swein say?" Moore asked.

"He gave me no help, even though we were of the same flesh."

"Ellie hasn't been trained in the Ancient Crafts," Moore said. The constable's voice was thoughtful. "And she's never been one of us, as you are."

"Swein is to blame for that," Belthane told him. Her voice had an angry edge. "I asked him often to let me bring her into the Craft so that the two of us could form a coupling, but he always said no."

"With Swein gone, who will train her?"

"I will, of course," Belthane insisted.

"You're sure that you can?" Moore asked. "Without Swein?"

"I'm sure. Remember, we have a blood bond, just as there was to hold Swein and me together, even after he began growing restless."

"In the end, we had to sacrifice Swein to protect our coven," Moore said thoughtfully. "Are you sure that we will not have to send Ellie to join Swein, if she doesn't accept our offer?"

"Then she must be sent to join Swein," Belthane replied.

Though Longarm had encountered many merciless individuals during his years as a lawman, the icy chill carried by Belthane's voice sent a shudder down his spine.

"Who will carry out the ritual, if we do?" Moore asked. "Ellie is of your blood. It would be—"

"My blood comes now from Iuvart and Baalbrith and Asteroth," Belthane told him. Her voice was harsh. "I will carry out the ritual. Remember, it will not be the first time."

There was no tinge of sympathy in her words, no trace of any human quality. As Longarm had listened to the conversation between Belthane and the constable, its chilling inhumanity had set his anger growing minute by minute. He kept it in check now, while he considered the best course to follow.

*Old son*, he told himself silently, *those people have to be crazy to act like they're doing, but crazy folks can do more damage in a minute than sane ones can in an hour. You better get to Ellie and find someplace where it'll be safe to put her for a little while. Then you can come back and clean up this mess you stepped into, because now you got a real good idea of what they're scheming up to do.*

Closing the door quietly, he started back through the cavern. He made no attempt to move silently now, or to conceal himself in the shadows of the cool stone passageway. It seemed to Longarm that the passage had grown longer and more torturous during the short time that had passed since he'd gone along it in the opposite direction, but at last he came to its end and pushed open the door to the constable's home.

Not bothering to close the door, he went up the stairs and through the deserted dwelling into the starlight. After the time he'd spent in the total darkness of the cavern, the night seemed bright in spite of the scudding bank of black clouds in the north that was pushing toward the low-hanging moon. The air was fresh and a fitful breeze was blowing. Longarm's horse was waiting where he'd left it. He swung into the saddle, reined the animal around the barn, and headed toward Salem and the doctor's house.

A light was showing from the parlor window, the only light that Longarm saw as he approached the little spread-out village. He pulled up, dismounted, and hurriedly looped his reins around the hitching post. He took a long step toward the door when the caution instilled from experience stopped him.

Turning back to the horse, he led the animal around the side of the house where it would be out of sight. Then he went to the door and rapped. After a moment, when there still had been no reply, he knocked again.

"I'm coming as fast as I can, Father!" Ellie's voice reached him distantly through the door. Then the key scraped in the lock, and the door opened. As it swung inward Ellie went on, "I forgot to take the key out of the lock so you could open it with yours. I'm—" She stopped short when she saw Longarm. "I was sure it was Father," she went on. "He still hasn't come home."

During his brief ride from Moore's house, Longarm had tried to think of a way to tell Ellie gently that her father was dead, but in spite of the number of times he'd done it in the past, he'd been unable to think what to say. He stretched the time left by suggesting, "Maybe I better come in and sit down with you for a minute, Ellie. There's some things I got to tell you."

"Something's happened, hasn't it?" she asked.

"A lot of things. But if it's all right with you, let's get indoors first. Then we can talk."

Ellie's face was sober now. She nodded and stepped aside to let Longarm enter, then closed the door and turned the key.

"I suppose we'd better go into the parlor," she told him. "That's where I've been sitting waiting, and it's the only room where I've lighted a lamp."

By the time they'd finished their short walk up the hall and settled into chairs, Longarm had still found no easy way to begin. Ellie broke the silence at last.

"Something bad has happened, hasn't it?" she asked. When Longarm nodded, she went on. "Father's dead, isn't he?"

"I'm afraid so," Longarm replied.

Ellie's expression had not changed, but strain showed in her voice as she went on, saying, "I guess you'd better tell me what happened, Marshal Long. I'm sure it has something to do with the way he's acted lately."

"I don't know all the ins and outs of what happened myself, yet, Ellie," he told her. "He was shot, but I don't know who did it or when. I aim to find out, but I figured you better hear about it first."

Frowning now, but her eyes still dry, she said, "If he'd been shot accidentally, you'd have told me right off. It wasn't an accident, was it?"

"I'm afraid not."

"He hasn't been in any arguments that I know of," Ellie said. "But it must be somebody here in Salem who killed him, even if I can't think why."

Longarm's mind felt relieved now that the worst part of his errand had been completed. He asked Ellie, "What were you talking about a minute ago when you mentioned your daddy hadn't been acting lately like he generally did?"

"I—he—" Ellie stopped and shook her head. "I can't put it in words, Marshal Long. I can't even think about it right straight."

"I don't like to prod at you, Ellie, but it'd sure help me if you'd try."

Ellie did not answer for a moment, then she said, "He began changing several months ago. He'd sit for a long time at the table while we were eating, only he didn't eat much or seem to enjoy what little he did eat. And sometimes he'd say he had to go make a house call, even when there hadn't been anybody come here looking for him. And—" She stopped and shook her head. "I don't know what else to tell you."

"He never did say anything about what was bothering him?"

"Not to me. But he was away from the house a lot. When he wasn't here, I think he spent most of his time with Uncle Perc."

"You mean the constable?"

Ellie nodded. "But there was something I still don't understand. Two or three times when he said he was going to see Uncle Perc, a patient came looking for him while he was away, and two times when the patients needed Father really seriously, I went out to Uncle Perc's house and there wasn't anybody there."

"Did you ask your daddy where they'd gone?"

"Yes, of course. And he said they'd ridden out on the prairie to get a breath of fresh air."

"And did you ask him anything else?"

Ellie shook her head. "No. It just stuck in my mind because Father never has liked to ride horseback. He had a buggy when I was a little girl, but it wore out and he never did get another one, just traded the old horse for a saddle horse and that's what he's been riding ever since, even if he kept saying he didn't like sitting in a saddle."

"So you—" Longarm broke off when a knock sounded at the outside door.

Ellie stood up, saying "I'll have to go see who it is. It may be somebody who needs—"

Before Ellie could finish, a man's voice came from the front door. "Ellie!" he called. "It's me, your Uncle Perc. Hurry up and let me in, I've got something nice to tell you!"

# Chapter 13

Ellie started for the door the moment she heard Moore's voice, but Longarm took her arm and stopped her.

"No, Ellie," he said. "I can't let you go to the door."

"Why on earth not? It's only Uncle Perc."

"I hate to have to tell you this, because I know you set a world of store by Constable Moore, but from what I've seen and found out, he's all tied in with whoever it was that killed your daddy."

Ellie's mouth opened but she said nothing while a frown of disbelief grew on her face. At last she found her voice.

"You must be mistaken, Marshal Long!" she gasped. "Why, Father and Uncle Perc were just like brothers! He'd be the last man on earth to do anything that would have harmed my father!"

"I know it's hard for you to believe," Longarm told her. "And I wish I didn't have to be the one to tell you, but I know for a fact it's true."

"You'll have to prove it to me, then! And I'm going to—" She broke off when Moore called again.

"Ellie, honey! I know you're in there! Hurry along now and open up this door for me!"

Ellie tried to move, but Longarm was still holding her arm. She said, "Marshal Long, please let me go! I've only known you for a few days, but I've known Uncle Perc since I was a baby, and I'd trust him anytime or anywhere!"

"Maybe you would, but I sure don't. Not after listening to him and some of the others plotting while they were down in that cave under his house."

"Cave?" she asked.

Longarm nodded. "The one where your daddy's dead body's laying right now, Ellie. And that's something else I got to tell you about your Uncle Perc. He might've been—" He was interrupted by the thudding of a heavy fist on the door.

Percival Moore's voice followed the knocking as it echoed through the hallway. "I'm getting real outa patience with you, Ellie!" There was anger instead of wheedling in his tone now. He went on, "What's got into you, girl? You know you don't have to be afraid of me! Hurry up and unlock the door!"

Ellie looked at Longarm. Even in the gloom he could see the perplexity on her face, and realized that she was being torn between the incomplete story that he, as a stranger, had told her, and the man outside, whom she'd grown up to love and trust since babyhood. He returned to the last argument that had occurred to him in a final effort to persuade her.

"I don't have a reason in the world to lie to you, Ellie," Longarm said. "But there's been a lot of things going on here in Salem that you don't know about."

"I guess I don't understand you," she said frowning. "What kind of things are you talking about?"

"Mostly ugly things, and your daddy could save you from them while he was alive. But that's all changed now that he's dead. Tell me just one thing. Did you ever hear your Uncle Perc talk to you before the way he is now?"

Ellie had been turning away from Longarm as he spoke. Now she looked back at him. For a moment she did not speak, then she said slowly, "No. I don't remember a time when Uncle Perc talked like he's been doing this evening."

"Then don't that tell you there's something really wrong?"

"I . . . I don't know what to believe, Marshal," she said slowly. "But Uncle Perc—"

Renewed hammering followed by the constable's voice at the front door interrupted her. "I'm giving you one more chance to open this door, girl!" Moore shouted. "Then I'm going to bust it down and come in after you! And you'll be sorry if you make me do that!"

"You've got to believe me, Ellie!" Longarm urged. He was reluctant to use force on her rather than persuasion. The success of the plan that had begun to take shape in his mind as he rode in from the cavern depended on Ellie's willing cooperation. He went on, "At least give me a chance to prove what I've been trying to tell you. If I'm wrong, all you've done is waste a little bit of time. As soon as you find out for yourself what I'm trying to save you from, you'll be glad you waited."

Even in the dim light Longarm could see reluctance on Ellie's face as she stood silent, still hesitant. Then the crash of Moore's booted foot against the front door broke the silence again. The wooden panel did not yield to his kick, and the heavy thudding was repeated.

"All you need to tell you that something's wrong is to listen to the way your Uncle Perc is trying to kick your front door down," Longarm said quickly.

"I, I guess you're right, Marshal Long," Ellied replied. There was still reluctance in her voice as she went on, "Even if I didn't understand at first that something's wrong, I do now. But I still don't know what it is."

"And there ain't enough time right this minute for me

to explain all the ins and outs of it," Longarm said. "All I can do is ask you to trust me."

"All right," she agreed. "What do you want me to do?"

"I reckon there's a back door we can get out of, without your Uncle Perc seeing us? My horse is behind the shed outside."

"There's a back door," she said. "Come on, I'll show you."

Before they'd reached the end of the hallway Moore's knocks began again. This time the tattooing thunkings of his fists came from the door that they were now approaching, and his knocking was accompanied by the metallic rattling of the doorknob.

"He's come around to the back door," Ellie said, and now there was an overtone of real worry in her voice. "I don't guess you want me to let him in, after what you've told me."

"No," Longarm replied quickly. Then without hesitating he took Ellie's arm and swung her around to reverse their direction. "We'll got out the front. You lock the door behind us and take the key with you."

As he spoke, Longarm's agile mind was carrying his still-unformed plan a step further. Ellie unlocked the front door as another burst of fist pounding echoed through the hallway from the rear of the house. Longarm stepped onto the porch and waited in the fast-gathering darkness while she locked the door from the outside, then took her arm and hurried her to the hitch post where Moore's horse was standing. In his haste, the constable had not hitched his mount, and its reins were still looped around the saddle horn.

"I reckon you can ride a horse?" Longarm asked Ellie.

"Why, of course!"

"Then get on this one," he told her, cupping his hands and bending forward.

Too confused by now to be anything except obedient, Ellie let him boost her into the saddle. Longarm took the reins and led the animal to the corner of the house. Stopping, he peered carefully around the angle and saw that his livery horse was standing placidly where he'd left it. Stepping up to the animal and grasping its reins with his free hand, Longarm listened for a moment to the constable's shouts and knocks at the back door of the house they'd just left. Then he turned the steed slowly and urged it ahead the short distance necessary for him to get a foot into its stirrup.

Longarm did not release the reins of the animal Ellie was riding, but led it as he toed his own mount ahead. They'd ridden only a short distance through the darkness when Ellie broke the strained silence that had fallen between them.

"Where are you taking me?" she asked.

"First of all, we have to find someplace where we can rest and talk," he replied. "Then after you get over being all mixed up like you are now, we'll figure out what to do. I imagine you'd know someplace close by where we can go without nobody being likely to stumble over us for a while?"

Ellie frowned as she asked, "What kind of place do you mean?"

"Oh, it don't have to be much. Maybe an old house that somebody's moved away from and left. Or a gully we can ride into where it ain't likely we'll be spotted. Even a good stand of trees or brush would do in a pinch if it grows pretty thick and tall enough to keep anybody from seeing our horses' rumps."

166

"I guess we could go to the old Pearson place," she offered. "It's not much over a mile away, but the road peters out before you get to it. There's not much left of the house, because it hasn't been lived in for so long. And there's a clump of cottonwoods around it that the first Pearsons planted when they built it. The trees are pretty high now. I don't suppose anybody'd see us, or even think we might go there, especially in the dark."

"That sounds about like what I got in mind," Longarm said. "Which way is it? And how far?"

"Maybe a mile past Uncle Perc's house."

"I reckon you can find it in the dark?"

"Of course, if that's where you want to go."

"It ain't that I want to, but it seems like it's where we got to go, whether we like it or not. You lead the way, then. Once we get there safe, I'll try to explain everything that's happened so you'll understand what all this fuss is about."

Following Ellie through the deepening gloom of onrushing night, Longarm rode close to her as she led the way along Salem's silent street toward the open prairie. The night was moonless, and the starshine had not yet overcome the gloom. Most of the little town's few houses were dark, though in a few of them thin slits of yellow lamplight gleamed through closed shutters.

They'd put the little settlement behind them when the thudding horses' hooves on the loose earth of the trail they were following broke the quiet air. A patch of darkness at one side of the road indicated some sort of brush and promised cover of a sort. Longarm touched the flank of his mount with the toe of his boot and led Ellie away from the trail. He reined his mount to a halt in the dubious shelter of the low clump of brush-created shadows and pulled Ellie's horse as close to his own as possible.

In a moment the rider behind them thudded past. Even in the darkness Ellie recognized the rider and whispered, "It's Uncle Perc."

"I sorta figured it might be," Longarm said. He looked toward the constable's house on the little rise, still some distance from the spot where he and Ellie sat. "And there ain't but one place he could be headed for."

"His house, of course," she said.

"And what's under the ground beyond it," Longarm added.

"I still can't understand why I've never heard about what you've said is under Uncle Perc's house, the cave and all that," Ellie said. "Just the idea of not knowing frightens me a little bit. And from what you've hinted, there are some things you haven't even told me yet, Marshal Long."

"I can't seem to find a place to start," Longarm replied. "But right now sure ain't the time to start talking about it. Soon as that constable gets a little ways in front of me, I aim to follow him into that cellar."

"What about me? Aren't you going to take me with you? I'd feel safer than I'd be out at the old Pearson place. It's sort of spooky at night."

Longarm was silent for a moment, then he asked, "I don't reckon you've got any kinfolk or real good friends you could stay with while I'm gone? Somebody you're sure you can trust?"

Ellie shook her head slowly. "Outside of Uncle Perc, about the only folks I'm acquainted with are Father's patients, and I don't know any of them very well."

"Then there's only one thing I can see to do, Ellie. Come on with me to the constable's house. He's got a big barn, and I don't imagine we'll have any trouble finding some place in it where you can hide and be safe."

Darkness had settled in full by the time they reached Moore's house. None of the windows showed telltale lights and the doors were all closed. With Ellie following closely, Longarm rode in a wide half-circle around the house and kept the big barn between them and the dwelling while they approached.

Inside, the darkness was even blacker. Longarm lit a match, and when his eyes had adjusted to the small glimmering light, surveyed the barn's cavernous interior. There were horses in three of four of the stalls, and beyond them, attached to the end wall, he saw the ladder leading to the hayloft and motioned toward it.

"It ain't likely that Moore's going up to pitch any hay down tonight, Ellie. You climb up that ladder and scrunch down in the hay. It don't matter what you see or hear, don't you dare move from it till I come back here and tell you it's safe."

Ellie nodded obediently and started toward the ladder that led to the hayloft. Longarm followed her, lighting another match and holding it until she'd scrambled up the ladder to the loft. Then he turned away and walked slowly toward Moore's darkened house.

Longarm still had no fixed plan of action for the moments that lay ahead. As he'd expected, the front door was locked, but the horse the constable had been riding stood at the hitch rail. Going to the back door, he tried it. As he'd hoped, it was unlocked, swinging from its hinges. Stepping quietly inside he scratched a match into light.

If anything had changed in the kitchen, Longarm could not tell it during the brief moment that passed before the flame of his match reached his fingertips and he blew it out. Moving by memory, he crossed the room to the stove and groped for the box of matches from which he'd replenished his supply earlier. He scooped up another handful, tucked them into his almost-empty vest pocket, and started for the half-open door which led to the underground passage.

This time the midnight blackness of the tunnel held no surprises for him. His earlier trips through the underground passageway had left in Longarm's retentive mind a map of each curve and slope of its winding course. When the last few glimmers of light faded and darkness took over, he no longer had to risk lighting matches to be sure of the course that lay ahead. He kept moving at a brisk pace, one hand slipping along the rocky striations of the cavern wall, the other free to reach for his Colt if some unexpected danger should be encountered ahead.

Without having to worry that a stray glimmer of light from the occasional match he struck or that the sudden scraping of his boot soles on an unexpectedly slippery stretch of floor might warn others of his approach, Longarm could move much more swiftly than he'd been able to on his earlier trips through the underground tunnel. Long before he reached the place where the cavern widened into the ceremonial chamber, even before he could see a wispy ray of light in the gloom ahead, he heard the muted sounds of voices ahead of him and moved more carefully.

When he began to make out words in the murmuring gabble of sounds, Longarm slowed his advance still more. At the point where he could see light glowing faintly in the tunnel ahead he moved with even greater caution, and strained his ears to make out words from what had been incomprehensible gibberish when he first heard the voices of the witchcrafters.

It was a man's voice that reached his ears, and though the voice was higher pitched and more rhythmic than it had been when he first heard it, by its hoarse timbre he recognized it as being that of Percival Moore. He could not make out the words themselves, for the constable was chanting in some strange tongue, by which Longarm quickly deduced that the members of the coven were engaged in one of their rituals or ceremonials.

As he advanced, the light grew steadily brighter, flickering occasionally, glowing yellowish, and now Longarm knew that it was coming from the same over-sized candle that had provided illumination earlier. Moving with even greater care than before, he edged along the wall until he could look into the wide portion of the cave occupied by Belthane's bed.

What he saw brought Longarm to a sudden halt. Constable Moore stood against the cavern wall, his eyes closed, his head thrown back while he chanted in the weird gibberishlike language that Longarm had heard the coven's members use before. One of the men of the coven—he could not see the man's face—was lying stretched out naked on the bed. Belthane was crouched on her hands and knees above him. She was also naked and behind her stood a second man, his unclothed body jerking convulsively as he threw back his head and joined the chant in rhythm with the constable.

Belthane lifted her torso just as Longarm took the final short step that allowed him to see the scene clearly. she was quivering, her full breasts swaying and gleaming with sweat as she raised her head and chimed into the chant that the constable and the naked man behind

171

her were raising. The man on the bed sat up and joined the others in the strange songlike mouthings. —

Longarm could not distinguish any of the words they used, and in spite of its rhythmic beat, the melody in which their voices were joining was one of unworldly eeriness. Then Belthane suddenly stopped chanting and loudly cried out a single word which Longarm did not understand. Whatever the word was, it stopped the others from chanting and drew their attention to her.

"Hurry!" Belthane said loudly. "Now, we are all of one body, and our strength is too great for mere humans to resist! Let us go and take the intruder who has learned our secrets and tonight we will assemble the full coven and appease Lughnasadah by sacrificing him!"

In that instant, while the coven's members were still motionless and unaware of his presence, Longarm realized the opportunity that had been handed him. He moved at once to take advantage of the chance.

"Just stay right where you are!" he commanded loudly, stepping away from the wall and into the candle-light. As he moved he drew his Colt and brought it up, swinging the blue steel barrel to cover the four in front of him. "All of you are under arrest! Now line up with your faces to that wall behind you while I fix it so you can't get away from me again."

One of the men started to move toward him, but before Longarm could swing his Colt to cover the moving man Belthane stopped his advance with a quick command.

"Obey him!" she said. "It is only for a short while. Our magic is not powerful enough to overcome his gun, but it is a human weapon. It cannot stand against the spell I will call forth from our own gods! Before daybreak he will be another to surrender his life to our quiet guns!"

"I'll take my chances on that," Longarm told her. "Now, all of you step back against that wall over yonder while I find something to tie you up with."

He gestured with the Colt's muzzle as he spoke. Belthane obeyed his command, and her followers moved slowly to line up beside her. Longarm flicked his eyes around the lighted area, looking for something that he could use as a rope. He saw nothing but the rumpled sheets on the bed and without allowing the muzzle of his weapon to waver, moved to the bed and with his free hand took his knife from his pocket and opened it.

Once again he was forced to use a makeshift rope. Without letting the Colt's muzzle waver or drop, Longarm nicked the bed sheet and tore it into strips. He tucked the ends of the strips into his belt and moved toward his prisoners.

"Turn your faces to the wall," he commanded. "And put your hands in back of you."

Silently, the four obeyed him, and four the next few minutes Longarm was busy juggling the Colt as best he could while he secured their wrists behind their backs. He'd left Belthane to tie up last, and ignored the suggestive wriggling of her bare hips and the swaying of her full breasts while he secured her wrists behind her. At last the job was finished and he stepped away from the cavern wall.

"Now, you four've got away with all sorts of things in this place," he said. "So just to make sure you don't get a chance to do any more scheming while I'm gone, I guess I better gag you, too.

Turning away, he holstered his Colt and stepped to the bed where he tore another strip from the already-ripped sheet. He'd gagged the constable and one of the men and was moving to the next man in line when a whisper of sound behind him reached his ears. Longarm started to turn, his hand going for his holstered Colt, when something hard and heavy crashed into his head. Blackness blanked his mind as he sagged and collapsed on the cave's stone floor.

# Chapter 14

Longarm opened his eyes and blinked to clear them before he became aware that the blackness surrounding him was real, and not the result of flawed vision. He started to shake his head, for he could hear nothing at all, but the movement brought a stabbing pain and he stopped moving at once.

Belatedly he realized that neither his eyes nor his ears were to blame for the total darkness and the utter silence, that he could neither see nor hear because he was still in the cave. The stabbing pain that he felt dancing in his head when he moved it did not go away when he lay quietly, but he wondered why he felt so uncomfortable whenever he tried to move.

His face felt chilled on one side and warm on the other, and only a moment after that sensation had made itself known he understood that he was lying cheekdown on the stone floor of the cavern where he'd interrupted the witches' ritual.

He tried to lift himself, but his legs refused to respond. Like his face, his legs were pressed against the chilly stone floor and the cold had stiffened his muscles, almost depriving them of feeling. When Longarm attempted to stretch his legs the ropes around his wrists grew taut and the muscles in his arms protested, but nothing else happened.

His hands also felt chilled, and his fingers seemed to have vanished, for he could not open or close his hands, nor did he get any sensation that they were moving. Then his memory came flooding back, and he realized where he was and what must have taken place.

*You got knocked out, old son,* Longarm said silently
as he made another futile effort to force his muscles to
function. *Then somebody hog-tied you. You're laid out
in that cave, and it's your own fool fault. There ain't
nobody else to blame it on. You was so set on tying up
them fellows who was with that Belthane, you forgot to
look in back of you. Now you got to figure out a way to
get loose before that witch and her men get back, or
you're going to be in real big trouble. Not that you ain't
already.*

Setting his jaw, Longarm began working at his
bonds. The darkness of the cavern prevented him from
seeing what he was doing, and he was fored to work
blind. The harsh fibers of the rough rope that shackled
his wrists scratched his skin painfully as he tried to
force some slack into its loops, and after a few tries he
stopping straining. He could feel fresh cold chills creeping down his fingers, and realized that the rough rope
had cut into his skin and started his wrists to bleeding.

*Now, that ain't going to help you one damn bit, old
son,* he told himself. *Whoever hog-tied you this way
sure as hell knew what he was doing. If you get your
wrists and hands all boogered up, you ain't going to be
able to handle a gun the way you need to. This mess
you're in right now needs brains to get out of, not mus-
cle.*

Longarm lay motionless for a few moments, trying to
relax as much as possible with the ropes that bound
him, holding him in what at best was an uncomfortable
position. Then he began trying again to free himself.
His efforts drew a bit more pain than that which had
accompanied his first attempts, with even less reward,
for by now his wrists were raw and each move seemed

176

to draw the bonds more deeply into his flesh.

He forced himself to relax again and was lying quietly when a whisper of motion reached his ears. Automatically, the sound triggered him into motion, but the biting of the rough rope fibers into his wrists warned him that he must stop or pay the consequences when and if he managed to get free. He let his muscles go lax. The pain eased and he strained to hear.

Once again he could hear the soft shushing noise. It seemed to be drawing closer. For a fleeting moment Longarm thought he saw a glinting of light at one side, but when he concentrated on staring into the murky black he decided that he'd been mistaken. Then he heard the unmistakable sound of a matchhead scratching and saw what seemed to his dark-expanded pupils to be a blinding light burst from the corridor of the cavern.

When the light stabbed into his eyes Longarm closed them instinctively, then opened them a slit. The light was closer now, flickering along the cavern walls. Then a woman's soft voice broke the silence, a whisper that sounded like a shout in the tomblike quiet.

"Marshal Long? Is that you I heard moving?"

Relief and caution kept Longarm silent for the fraction of a second that brought him the realization that if Ellie had made her way unmolested through the depths of the cavern they must be alone in the witches' underground retreat. Then he answered her question.

"It's me, Ellie," he said. "And you've got no idea how glad I am to see you. I guess we're by ourselves down here right now, so come on ahead. I'm all tied up, but I reckon you can get me loose."

As he spoke the light flickered and vanished, but another match scratch brought the brilliance back with a flaring sputter that settled into a steady glow and grew brighter as Ellie approached. By the time she'd reached him, her match had burned out and she lit still another.

"You'd best hurry," Longarm cautioned her. "I don't know how long that Belthane and her men have been gone, but they could be getting back any time."

"Belthane?" Ellie frowned as she dropped to her knees at Longarm's side and held her flickering match high to inspect his bonds. "Who's that?"

"Never mind," Longarm replied quickly as he realized that Ellie knew nothing of her twin sister. "We can talk about that later on, after we get outside. I got a pocketknife in my jeans that'll cut these ropes, if you can get to it."

Twisting to lie on his face, Longarm indicated with a nod the side pocket which held his knife. Ellie slid her hand into it and found the knife, opened it, and began sawing at the rope that was twisted cruelly tight around his wrists. After a few moments the fettering strands loosened and fell away. Longarm reached for the knife, but his stiff swollen fingers fumbled it and let it fall.

"I guess you better finish the job," he told her, nodding at the strands which still bound his ankles.

While Ellie picked up the knife and started working on the rope, Longarm fumbled one of his long thin cigars from his vest pocket and lit it. Under Ellie's work with the sharp blade of his knife, the rope with which he'd been bound gave way quickly, and in a moment Longarm was free. He started to stand up, but his numbed legs gave way and with a thud he settled back to the stone floor.

"Give me a minute or two," he said, taking another drag from his cigar. "I guess I been tied up longer'n I figured, but I'll be all right soon as I get some feeling back in my legs. How'd you happen to find me, Ellie?"

"Well, I waited and waited," she replied. "Just like you told me to do, in Uncle Perc's barn. Then all of a sudden I heard a lot of commotion and talking, and some men came in the barn and got the horses. They were talking, too, but all I could get from what they said was that they were in a hurry. When they left with the horses, I peeked through a crack in the wall and watched them ride off."

Ellie stopped, frowning as the match she was holding burned to her fingertips, and took another from her pocket. Holding it in the flame of the one that was flaring out, she waited until the fresh sliver of wood was burning steadily, then went on.

"I couldn't see much through the crack, Marshal Long, but I think one of the ones who rode away was a woman."

"You got good eyes," Longarm said. "But we don't have time to waste in here, just standing talking. Let's get back to your house, and when we find a place that's safe, I'll tell you the whole story. Maybe after you hear it, all this will make sense to you."

Striking a fresh match each time the one that she was holding burned too short to hold, Ellie walked beside Longarm through the cavern. Longarm did not draw her attention to the body of her father, no longer covered by the bloodstained, bullet-torn quilt at one side of the passageway. They passed through the area where the walls expanded to form Belthane's bedroom and the meeting place of the witches' coven, and were climbing the steps from Constable Moore's cellar into his house when they heard the thud of hoofbeats approaching.

"That's likely them coming back," Longarm said. "But we just might be able to get to the barn if we hurry. Come on, Ellie! Let's try!"

Even before they reached the door between Moore's kitchen and the living room, the sound of the approaching riders was so loud that Longarm realized they had only a slight chance of reaching the barn safely.

"We'd be cut down like sitting ducks if we stay in here, Ellie," he said. "But if we can get to my horse, I'll have my rifle and plenty of shells in my saddlebags, which'll give us a good chance to hold 'em off. I'll stay here and slow 'em down. They're not likely to see you in the dark, so you cut a streak to the barn, and I'll be there soon as I get a chance."

"But I hate to—"

"Don't argue!" Longarm said sternly. "Just keep the house between you and them riders as much as you can and get back up in the hayloft! Move, now!"

There was an urgency in Longarm's voice that warned Ellie not to protest. She turned at once and started for the barn. Longarm watched her running through the darkness for a moment, his ears peaked to catch the hoofbeats of the approaching riders, then he turned and stepped to the window, his Colt drawn and ready.

As he'd suspected, the coven had gone for reinforcements, probably into Salem. Their mission had been at least partly successful, for there were six riders galloping toward the farmhouse. Belthane rode in the lead, her long black hair and gossamer robe streaming behind her and shimmering in the fading moonlight. Because of the darkness, Longarm could not identify any of the other riders except Constable Moore, who was galloping at the side of the group and a short distance ahead of his companions.

For a moment, Longarm debated with himself about being the first to shoot, but his lawman's habits were too ingrained. He did not spend a lot of time in thought before stepping to the window. It was closed, and after fumbling for a moment while the approaching coven drew closer he shattered the glass with a blow from his Colt.

"You people stop right where you are!" he shouted "My name's Custis Long. I'm a deputy United States marshal, and I'm arresting the whole bunch of you! Just put down your guns and surrender peaceful!"

"Don't listen to him!" Belthane shrieked. "He is the enemy of all our kind! Kill him!"

A shot sounded from the straggled-out riders and the shrill whine of a lead slug ended with a thunk as the bullet splintered the window frame only inches from Longarm's head. He held his fire, looking toward the spot where he'd seen the red streak of muzzle blast. Even in the darkness Longarm could identify the rider. The man who'd fired was Constable Moore.

Dropping to one knee beside the window, Longarm triggered his Colt. Moore's rifle cracked almost at the same instant. The bullet whistled through the broken window and buried itself harmlessly in the wall behind Longarm.

Before Moore could fire again, Longarm's lead went true. The constable's rifle fell from his hands and he swayed for a moment in the saddle, then lurched forward and toppled from his mount, falling to the ground in a motionless huddle.

Another rifle shot cut the night air and burning powder spurted red from the muzzle of another horseman's rifle. The slug shrilled uncomfortably close to Longarm's ear, then went home into the shelf of a cabinet that stood along the back wall, raising a clatter and clinking of broken china from the stack of plates into which it had crashed.

Longarm fired at the muzzle flash, as he'd done so often before when facing a band of night riders. Though he'd taken no time to aim, his experience as a seasoned veteran of many such clashes made his shooting almost automatic. The range had closed now, and his Colt had become as effective as the attackers rifles. The man in the saddle of the galloping horse lurched when the revolver's slug took him in the chest, and like the constable, he sagged and slid from the galloping horse to lie prone and motionless on the ground.

By now the remaining riders were beginning to converge on the house. As they drew closer they began shooting, their rifle-fire erratic but effective. Longarm dropped to the floor, and before returning the fire thumbed the cases of the two revolver shells he'd spent out of the Colt's cylinder and replaced them with fresh cartridges from his coat pocket.

He heard a shot from behind him, and an answering yell from one of the riders, who called, "There's somebody shooting from the barn now!"

Longarm understood at once that Ellie had found his rifle and made the most of the momentary distraction of his adversaries. Rising to his knees, he swept the scene in front of the cottage with an eye skilled by experience. Then he got off one shot, followed immediately by another. His two targets toppled from their saddles and lay still.

Two more shots sounded from the barn, bringing a yell from the single man who was galloping full tilt toward the corner of the house trying to reach Ellie's stronghold. Longarm fired once at the galloping target and missed, but his second shot went home. The rider dropped his rifle as he bounced out of the saddle and plunged to the sod, where he lay unmoving in an ungainly sprawl.

Only one rider besides Belthane remained. He was within a dozen yards of the window when he fired at its blackness, where Longarm kneeled behind the sill. The windblast of his speeding bullet brushed Longarm's cheek as it sang past him with a high-pitched menacing whine.

Longarm did not flinch. He was swiveling his Colt as the hot lead cutting the air brushed past his cheek. Before the oncoming rider could lever another shell into his rifle's chamber, Longarm triggered off the fatal shot. The horseman's Winchester, its breech still open, dropped from his lifeless hands as the Colt's bullet went home.

As the horseman fell, the rifle got entangled with the hind legs of his galloping mount. Weapon, animal, and man hit the ground as one in an ungainly sprawl. The rider lay still, but the horse struggled to its feet and galloped off, its shrill neighing a mingling of anger, fear, and hurt as its hooves thudded on the hard soil.

In the sudden silence that had returned to the night, Longarm looked for Belthane. His eyes found her at last. She was standing a yard or so away from her horse, near the place where Constable Moore lay sprawled in death. Longarm could not make out her features, but he could see the small white columns of her uplifted arms, and the pale oval of her face.

Belthane began chanting. Her voice reached Longarm clearly, but the words of her singsong intonations were in a language that he did not understand. Then she began swaying to the strange rhythms of her song and she spread her arms wide as she twirled slowly, the full-cut sleeves of her robe fluttering as she turned. At each of the four points of the compass she stopped for a brief moment to make a sweeping bow.

Transfixed by the strange sight, still tense from the gunfight so recently ended, Longarm stared at the slowly moving woman. He saw her drop her arms and let them rest for a moment while she continued her weird chant. She raised them again, and now he caught the glitter of starshine on the long knife she'd taken from her belt as she brought up her arms.

Before Longarm could call out or move, Belthane brought the glittering knife-blade down into her breast. Her chant trailed off to a sobbing sigh that ululated for a moment in the still night air and then diminished to nothingness. In the silence that now took the night, she crumpled into a small white heap on the ground and lay still.

Belthane's collapse broke the spell that had held Longarm fascinated and motionless. He vaulted through the shattered window and hurried to where she'd fallen. Even in the darkness a glance was enough to tell him that Belthane was dead. One of the full-cut arms of her dress trailed away from her. Longarm bent and pulled the fabric up to cover Belthane's face.

Even the soft footsteps that Longarm heard now sounded loud in the suddenly quiet night. He turned to see Ellie coming from the house. She was still carrying his Winchester.

"Are you all right, Marshal Long?" she asked as she came within speaking distance.

"I'm fine. Didn't get a scratch," he answered.

"There was so much shooting and horses galloping around that I stayed in back of the house for a while after all the noise stopped," Ellie went on. She glanced at the white heap on the ground a short distance from Longarm's feet and frowned, then asked, "Who on earth is that?"

"It's the woman who bossed them others that called theirselves witches, Ellie. I guess there wasn't as many of them as I figured." When Ellie leaned forward to get a closer look, Longarm put his hand on her shoulder and turned her gently toward the house. "Let's you and me go inside. Maybe we can find the makings for a pot of coffee. Then after we've rested for a little bit, I'll take you home."

"But what about..." Ellie seemed to run out of words as she indicated Belthane's body and swept her hand to include the others who lay scattered around the house. "And Father, too. Shouldn't we do something about—"

"I'll come back after a while and take care of whatever's got to be done," he promised her. "You've been upset for such a long time, I figure the best thing for you to do is crawl in bed and get some sleep."

"You need sleep, too," she said.

"Shucks, Ellie, in my job a man's got to stay up so many nights when he's on a case that I've plumb got used to it. Now, come along and let's get that coffee started."

Longarm walked into Billy Vail's office without knocking and laid a single sheet of paper on the heaped stacks of file-folders and creased envelopes that covered the top of the chief marshal's desk.

Vail looked up from the littered desk, then picked up the sheet of paper Longarm had added to the litter and scanned it quickly.

"I think this is the shortest report you've ever turned

185

in, Long," he said. Then he read aloud from the paper:
"'Case of stolen Indian Bureau money closed, sent to
Judge Parker. Case of Joseph alias One-finger Carter
closed by prisoner's death.' Now, just what kind of report do you call this? Where are the details?"

"Billy," Longarm said earnestly, "even if I was to
write twenty pages on them two cases you wouldn't believe a word of what I put down. And while I'm thinking of it, will you do me a favor?"

"Of course. If I can, that is."

"If you ever get a case that says anything about folks
being shot with quiet guns," Longarm said earnestly,
"give it to one of the other deputies, will you? I reckon
I've heard the last quiet gun go off that I'll ever want
to."

Watch for

**LONGARM IN THE VALLEY OF DEATH**

one hundred and fifteenth novel in the bold
LONGARM series from Jove

*coming in July!*

F